Theaker's Quarterly Fiction #51

Edited by
Stephen Theaker
and John Greenwood

Other titles from this publisher and related entities

Theaker's Quarterly Fiction #51

Edited by
Stephen Theaker
and John Greenwood

Cover Artist

Howard Watts

Contributors

Jacob Edwards
Walt Brunston
Marshall Moore
Howard Phillips
Andrea M. Pawley
Douglas J. Ogurek
Charles Wilkinson
Antonella Coriander

ISBN (print): 978-1-910387-07-8
ISBN (epub): 978-1-910387-08-5

ISSN (print): 1747-6083
ISSN (online): 1747-6075

Website: www.theakersquarterly.blogspot.com

Email: theakersquarterlyfiction@gmail.com

Lulu Store: www.lulu.com/silveragebooks

Feedbooks: www.feedbooks.com/userbooks/tag/tqf

Submissions: Submissions are very welcome! See website for guidelines and terms.

Advertising: We welcome ad swaps with small press publishers and other creative types, and we'll run ads for relevant new projects from former contributors.

Sending material for review: We are interested in reviewing almost anything that's fantasy-related. We prefer to receive books for review in epub or mobi format. Feel free to send ebooks without querying first. We have reviewed about 14% of items received, though many of those reviewed are things we've actively requested.

Mission statement: The primary goal of *Theaker's Quarterly Fiction* is to keep going. We need a new secondary goal, since we have not only caught up with *McSweeney's* but overtaken them (in issue numbers if not yet in fame).

Published in Theaker's Paperback Library
on 17 April 2015.

Contents

Editorial

Stephen Theaker

Small Changes in This Issue

Hi chums! You know that I love to experiment with this magazine. It's our *raison d'être*! We rarely go more than a few issues without changing X or tweaking Y or totally mucking up Z, W and V. The changes this time will mainly be invisible to you, in that I'm typesetting each section of the zine in a separate file, to make it simpler to get bits finished as I go along. That's been so successful that a good deal of this issue was ready to be published before issue fifty!

Where you might notice a change is in the Quarterly Review, which, again to break the work up a bit, I've redivided into categories, the way it used to be up until #46 (only this time, invisibly to you, each category is a separate file). I've also done something that pains me greatly: the reviews are no longer in alphabetical order... It's for the same reason: when a review comes in, from Jacob, or Douglas, or me, I can typeset it, put the cover image in place, proofread it, and then know those pages are finished.

My Reading in 2014

I read 144 books in total during 2014, according to my Goodreads list, which I try to keep fairly accurate. That comes down to 138 if we leave out books listed on there that I produced myself: *Theaker's Quarterly Fiction*, the *BFS Journal*, books from work. So that's a book about every three days, although I read an awful lot very quickly in December, and especially over Christmas, thanks to lots of Dark Horse comics becoming extremely cheap in the run-up to Marvel taking over the Star Wars licence.

I read 92 comics and 43 book-books, and there are 3 audiobooks on the list. I listened to more audiobooks than that, but I don't note dramas, Radio 4 comedies and things like that on Goodreads, just books. 116 of the books I read were ebooks of one kind or another: pdfs, Kindle, epub, Comixology. 19 were paper books, but not one of those was a full-length novel. 3 were digital (Audible) audiobooks. A lot of the prose books I read were very short: novellas, pocket books, Penguin Mini Moderns, etc. I only read about 26 full-length books last year, just one a fortnight, two-thirds of them review copies.

113 of the books I read were written or edited by men, and just 25 by women. Of the 3 audiobooks, all were written by men, but the inequality stems mainly from the comics I read. Of the 92 comics, 88 were edited or written by men, and just 4 by women. When it comes to the 43 prose books, 21 were written or edited by women, and 22 by men.

43 of the books I read in 2014 were originally published that year, while 19 came out in 2013, 13 in 2011, 9 in 2012, 10 in 2010. Reading books for review, and access to NetGalley, especially, seems to have brought my reading much more up-to-date than it used to be. The oldest books were *The Exploits of Engelbrecht* and *The Delicate Prey* from 1950. The newest was *The Glorkian Warrior Eats Adventure Pie*, due out in April 2015.

How did I get the books? I bought 95, 30 were

review copies, and 13 were Christmas and birthday presents. Of those I bought, 46 were on Kindle, 36 were from Comixology, 6 were print books purchased from Amazon, 4 were in Humble Bundles (or that kind of thing), 2 were from the Weightless Books shop, and one was bought direct from the publisher (*Billy's Book* by Terry Bisson). 3 of the review copies came via Audible, 21 from NetGalley, and 6 came directly from the publishers.

All my reading added up to roughly (very roughly – the page count is one of the least accurate parts of the Goodreads database) 27,125 pages: 8,923 pages of prose, 17,103 of comics, and the equivalent of about 1,099 pages in audio. Some of those will be books I began in previous years and only finished in 2014, but there are others I began in 2014 and didn't finish then, so it probably evens out. Thus I read about 24pp of prose a day over the course of 2014, and about 46pp of comics (two issues or so), amounting to about 74pp a day when the audiobooks are included.

It wasn't a year for long books. The longest I read was the *Archie 1000 Page Comics Bonanza* – not exactly a taxing read! – and next after that was *Showcase Presents: Superman Family, Vol. 3*, at 576pp. Nothing else topped five hundred pages. The shortest book on the list was *Suddenly, Zombies*, listed at 25pp.

I gave five stars to five books, which is a lot for me in a single year: *American Elf 2012* by James Kochalka, *Drunk with Blood* by Steve Wells, *The Etymologicon* by Mark Forsyth, *The Clockwork Muse* by Eviatar Zerubavel and *The Gifts of War* by Margaret Drabble. 30 books got four stars, so I read a lot of good stuff. 91 books got three stars, 7 got two stars, and just one book got one star from me: *Deadpool Classic, Vol. 1*. There were four unrated books; I try not to rate books on Goodreads till they're out. My average rating was

3.23. The average rating by other people on Goodreads for the same set of books was 3.87.

Who were my favourite authors last year? I'm just going on the first author listed on Goodreads, which can be a bit random with comics, but Mike Mignola comes top with 12 books read, thanks to all those cheap Dark Horse books on Kindle. Then James Kochalka with 5, and Matthew Hughes, Phil Hester, Dave Land (editor of *Star Wars Tales*) and Grant Morrison, all with 3 each. I read two books each from Elizabeth Bear, Andrew Chambliss, Danielle Corsetto, Matt Fraction, René Goscinny, Scott Gray, Adam P. Knave, Frank Miller, Alan Moore, Eric Powell, Rick Remender, Chris Roberson and Joss Whedon. There were then 83 writers by whom I read a single book. I tend to think of myself as finding new favourite authors and then reading them to exhaustion, but my reading last year seems to have been more varied than that.

Top-read publisher for me in 2014 was Dark Horse (33 books), followed by Marvel (9), IDW (6), Image and Top Shelf (5), DC and BOOM! (4). I read three each by Archie Comics, Asterix (according to Goodreads, at least), KaBOOM!, Puffin, Tor and Vertigo, and two each by Angry Robot, BBC Books, Cheeky Frawg Books, Del Rey, Hodder & Stoughton, Jo Fletcher Books, Panini, Penguin, PS Publishing, Subterranean Press, Top Cow Productions and 2000 AD.

I added 118 other books to my Goodreads list in 2014 that I haven't finished reading yet, from *The Complete Western Stories of Elmore Leonard* on January 4 to *Star Wars: Legacy, Vol. 11 – War* on December 31, so I'm in no danger of running out. About 70 of those were books I bought for myself, often cheaply in sales or sets. As far as hobbies go, reading isn't that expensive, but it seems daft to buy so many. Makes me feel like a hoarder, which, when it comes to books, I probably am. If I didn't read a single full-length paper novel last year, why have I still got hundreds of them in the house?

Apart from that, I don't really want to change anything for 2015. It'd be nice to read more comics by female writers. I'm looking forward to reading lots of the Penguin Little Black Classics. Print books will continue to drift further off the map. I'm finding pdfs a bit of a chore, now that proper ebooks are so often available, so that's begun to affect how much I read and review by some publishers. I hope NetGalley continues to thrive, but even if it doesn't, I've got plenty to keep me going. According to my Goodreads list, I've read 2,956 books, but 1,348 remain unread, 138 remain unfinished, and another 201 languish in hope of being read for review.

Contributors

Andrea M. Pawley's spirit animal is the piranhamoose. Hear her burble-roar at www.andreapawley.com.

Antonella Coriander has a plan, but she isn't saying what it is yet. Her story in this issue, "Cybertronica", is the fifth episode of her ongoing Oulippean serial, *Les aventures fantastiques de Beatrice et Veronique*.

Charles Wilkinson's story in this issue is "Water Imperial", about the peculiar goings-on at the Imperial Spa Hotel and Conference Centre. His publications include *The Pain Tree and Other Stories* and *Ag & Au*. His stories have appeared in *Best Short Stories 1990*, *Best English Short Stories 2*, *Midwinter Mysteries*, *Unthology*, *London Magazine*, *Able Muse Review*, and in genre publications such as *Supernatural Tales*,

Phantom Drift, Horror Without Victims, The Sea in Birmingham, Sacrum Regnum, Rustblind and Silverbright and *Shadows & Tall Trees*. New short stories are forthcoming in *Ninth Letter* and *Bourbon Penn*.

Douglas J. Ogurek's work has appeared in the *BFS Journal, The Literary Review, Morpheus Tales, Gone Lawn*, and several anthologies. He lives in a Chicago suburb with the woman whose husband he is and their five pets. This time he reviews *The Hobbit: The Battle of the Five Armies*. His website can be found at: www.douglasjogurek.weebly.com.

Howard Phillips is a dissolute poet whose contributions to this zine have ranged from the mediocre to the abysmal. In this issue he continues his latest autobiographical tale, *A Dim Star Is Born*, in "The Assassin's Lair". The previous instalment received such bad reviews that he wept for three days, burned seventeen unpublished novels, and wrote a series of angry blog posts accusing various parties of disparaging his genius. We asked him why he had taken it so badly, and he replied, "If you need to ask, you'll never know."

Howard Watts is a writer, artist and composer living in Seaford who provides the cover art for this issue. His artwork can be seen in its native resolution on his deviantart page: http://hswatts.deviantart.com. His novel *The Master of Clouds* is now available on Kindle.

Jacob Edwards flies with Australia's speculative fiction flagship *Andromeda Spaceways Inflight Magazine*, but meets us in the pub between runs. This writer, poet and recovering lexiphanicist's website is at www.jacobedwards.id.au. He also has a Facebook page at www.facebook.com/JacobEdwardsWriter, where he posts poems and the occasional oddity. Like him and follow him! In this issue he reviews *The Forever Watch* by David Ramirez, *Space Battleship Yamato* and *The Hobbit: The Battle of the Five Armies*.

Marshall Moore makes his TQF debut in this issue with "Too Much Light Makes the Day Go Blind". He is the author of four novels (*Bitter Orange, An Ideal for Living, The Concrete Sky* and *Murder in the Cabaret Sauvignon*) and three short-fiction collections (*The Infernal Republic, Black Shapes in a Darkened Room*, and the forthcoming *A Garden Fed by Lightning*). With Xu Xi, he is the co-editor of the anthology *The Queen of Statue Square: New Short Fiction from Hong Kong*. In addition to his work as an author, he is the principal at Typhoon Media Ltd, an independent publishing company based in Hong Kong, and he is a PhD candidate in Creative Writing at Aberystwyth University in Wales. For more information, see www.marshallmoore.com.

Stephen Theaker's reviews have appeared in *Black Static, Interzone, Prism* and the *BFS Journal*, as well as clogging up our pages. He shares his home with three slightly smaller Theakers, runs the British Fantasy Awards, and works in legal and medical publishing.

Walt Brunston's story in this issue is "One Slough and Crust of Sin", his adaptation of issue two of *The Two Husbands*. We don't know where he got those comics – apparently he's got the full run. We've never been able to find them in the UK. He's said that if we ever cross the pond he'll let us stay over and read them, but they have guns in the USA, and no NHS, which seems to us a remarkably dangerous combination.

Too Much Light Makes the Day Go Blind

Marshall Moore

The bright side of the Moon had never needed a name for itself. Nor did it realise its dreamlike consciousness did not extend all around and through, inside and out. Its self-awareness remained in a fog, only coming into focus as humanity quickened, asked questions, and launched rockets. When the Americans arrived and planted a flag, a clarity emerged. It still thought of itself as one entity, something of an enigma to itself but quite fortunate to have such a fascinating neighbour to help the time pass.

When a voice from the side of itself it considered its ass spoke up for the first time, the Moon almost exploded in shock and wiped out humanity. "Can you hear me?" asked the mystery. "Are you paying attention?"

Apollo 11 had barely departed. The bright side, struggling not to panic, could still feel the footprints Neil Armstrong and Buzz Aldrin had left on its scalp, and the scorch marks of their departure. They tingled.

"Where are you?" the Moon asked in its creaking, tectonic language.

"I'm what you'd call your dark side. The one you can't see."

The Moon tried to look. Lacking a mirror or any cosmic reflective equivalent, it couldn't see its own backside. It wasn't the Earth that was speaking: ill as the planet was, distracted by the damage wrought by humans, she rarely had much to say. She was too busy trying to wipe them out with hurricanes and plagues. Besides, people were far more intriguing. With their endless wars and complications, their discoveries and setbacks, the Moon had plenty to look at.

I have an id, the Moon mused, its terror subsiding.

"I'm a Jungian," said the voice after a long interval of contemplation. Its voice was a subtle idiom that echoed through the basalt of their shared being.

"But *who* are you?" the Moon asked.

"I'm your shadow. I'm you, but I'm not. And I'm leaving," said the voice.

"But that isn't possible. If you're me, and I'm one thing... a leg doesn't tell the body it's going to go its own way. Fingers and hands don't split up unless there's a blade."

"There's someone else," said the shadow.

The Moon felt a pang of regret for the loss of its blissful ignorance, and wished for a few weeks that it could slip back into unknowingness.

"Can we not talk about this now?" asked the Moon. "This is too new to me. I need some time to think."

The lack of an answer implied assent, so the Moon did what it did best: it eavesdropped. On the Earth. For centuries, it had heard lines like the one it had just delivered; it had never expected to need to use one, much less on what it thought of as a part of itself. If there was a solution, to be sure it would be found down below.

It listened in on the internet and on TV broadcasts, on private conversations and radio talk shows. It spied on the spy agencies whose personnel were reading their own countrymen's emails and intercepting their phone calls in the name of national security. Only when it had the idea to eavesdrop on the space agencies did the full picture begin to emerge.

"This would be a disaster. You can't do this – you can't separate from me. It's not physically possible!"

"Actually, it is," said the dark voice.

"We're a single, solid object."

"Not for long."

This would have chilled the Moon to its core if such a thing had still been possible. It listed its frigidity among its shortcomings and sometimes wondered whether swapping its near-eternal place in the firmament for the fleshly ability to fuck like a human, with all the concomitant pleasure and intrigue, might be worth it. A solid object, not for long?

"I told you there's someone else. And he's coming for me."

This confirmed all the Moon's worst suspicions. Astronomers on Earth had detected alarming irregularities in the orbit of Phobos, the larger of Mars's two moons.

"Phobos is going to crash into Mars and disintegrate into a pile of rubble. Scientists have known that for years."

"He's no longer suicidal. I've given him a reason to live. Or at least not to be so terrified of impact. When he crashes into us, the collision will set me free."

"But we'll all be destroyed in the process."

"So will your precious humanity down there on your big-sister planet that barely knows you exist, and good riddance. We prefer to think of it as transformation, not destruction. The more likely outcome is that there'll be three of us, not just two. We may orbit the Earth together, maybe we'll go back to Mars, or maybe we'll take up a space in the asteroid belt. Ceres is lovely. You'd like her."

"What can I give you to stay? I'll do anything."

"Can you rotate?"

The Moon hesitated.

"I thought so," said the darkness.

Desperate, the Moon sent messages down to the Earth to beg for some kind of intervention or at least another visit. There is, after all, a big difference between being looked at and being relevant. But these attempts at communication were misinterpreted as sunstorm interference. Zapped satellites fell on cities and into the sea; the obliteration of Berlin and Vladivostok would have made headlines around the world had the internet not massively short-circuited in the aftermath. The Moon sent a frantic call to Mars: *Change your gravity! Have work done! Do something – Phobos is deserting you!* The response was an indifferent: *Finally. He was just an asteroid I picked up, a hookup who wouldn't leave. He can fuck off and so can you.*

Even though the dark side had imposed no ultimatum, the Moon felt the clock ticking. The mystery might be willing to give it some time to sort things out, but it wouldn't wait forever. And the Moon could feel the change in Phobos's orbit, a subtle realignment. He was coming.

The panicking Moon turned elsewhere for help. Venus had a reputation for being wise about matters of love, but she rebuffed him. For one thing, she was on the opposite side of the Sun and couldn't be bothered. A nasty being, she'd grown gassy and irate in her old age, all carbon dioxide for an atmosphere and sulfuric acid for a personality. The asteroids the Moon begged for help were incredulous.

"You want us to kill ourselves in kamikaze raids on Phobos in hopes of changing his trajectory?" said Ceres, their ringleader. "Anyway, you do realise, I've just been promoted. I'm a dwarf planet now. You don't get to speak to me that way."

So much for lovely.

The Sun was similarly disinclined to help, as it would involve going supernova. Too massive to care about the fate of the inner planets and their inhabitants, its only concern was longevity.

"You got yourself into this," it scolded. "Get yourself out of it. Or just accept the inevitable."

Down on Earth, scientists had cancelled their plans for lunar colonies and sounded the alarm about Phobos. Based on their calculations, independently confirmed a dozen times over, the Martian satellite's departure from its orbit looked like the end of the human race. Not even the worst of the super-weapons people had dreamt up to hasten their own demise stood a chance of budging Phobos off its Earthward trajectory. The only saving grace would, of course, be the Moon itself... but even that came with its perils, as the Earth would be bombarded with debris from the collision. No matter what, humanity was fucked. The only question was timing. Phobos appeared to be moving much more slowly than an incoming asteroid, which meant there was time to prepare. Having no habitable alternative, humanity burrowed, and in the space of a couple of decades had largely moved deep underground in anticipation of a catastrophic rain of burning rocks.

The Moon could still hear them but had little to look at. It took a bittersweet satisfaction in knowing people and animals would escape the coming devastation, but having nothing left to watch was beyond depressing.

"Are you there?" asked the dark side one day.

The Moon was almost happy to hear from it.

"For now. Until Phobos destroys us, at least. What do you want?"

"To ask if you understand yet."

This annoyed the Moon to no end. "Understand

what? What is there to understand? You came to life, found a lover, and are going to have us all destroyed."

"I'm your archetype. I'm your shadow. I'm what you're capable of. And none of this would have happened if you'd been paying attention," said the mystery. "This is the last time you'll hear from me... until after."

In absolute despair, the Moon considered a fatal plunge into the Sun, which would put everyone concerned out of their misery. Was Phobos smitten enough to pursue its shadowy, pockmarked lover into the fire? It was such an enticing question that the Moon almost wanted to do it, just to find out. But something like sanity prevailed, and the Moon considered plotting a course for one of the outer planets. It could roam out into the Oort Cloud, which seemed to have plenty of room, and make a home for itself in the solar system's frigid outer suburbs. There was plenty of precedent for that down on Earth, and Sedna probably needed a friend.

A habit calcified over billions of years is a tough one to break. The Moon ruled out detaching itself from its orbit and rolling out into interstellar space, and alternate universes were simply too complicated. Human brains were difficult enough to contend with; branes were altogether beyond it.

With oblivion the only alternative, it reconsidered its ass and its axis, and turned.

"One Slough and Crust of Sin"

The Two Husbands #2

Walt Brunston

No one in the bank dares to look up at the man waving the gun around and yelling.

"Bring me the money!" he shouts. "Bring it to me right now!"

You can understand why they don't dare to look up at him. They are lying on the ground, and he has already said that he will kill anyone who moves a muscle. Why take the risk?

And yet... This man is unusual. They saw as much in the seconds before he told them to hit the ground. And none of them can quite believe it.

There is a tortoise in his head.

That may sound like an odd way to put it, but in fact it is totally accurate. His skull has been extended by about fifteen centimetres to create room for the tortoise. Its wizened head sticks out of a window in his forehead. Its upper shell covers the top of his head. By combining his own life with that of a tortoise, this man has extended his life by innumerable decades.

His name: Tortoisio.

And he is dangerous. Especially for these people in the bank. Because he might kill them if he doesn't get the money.

What are you going to do about it? How can you save these people? Keep reading, that's what! Just keep reading! It'll give the Two Husbands time to arrive!

"Where is my money, you poltroons?" he yells. "I have a gun in my hand. I made it myself. If you don't bring me any money I am going to start shooting. Some of you will die, but that is the least of my gun's unusual effects. You don't want to know the rest."

A middle-aged man who works at the bank sticks up an arm, as tentatively as possible. "Sir!" he whispers. "Sir!"

Tortoisio walks over to him and pokes the gun into the small of his back. The gun appears to be made from a carved potato, a length of copper wire, and a sealed pack of playing cards. Who knows what a gun like that could do?

"What is it?" asks Tortoisio. "And before you answer, consider that the grim reaper himself now watches you with interest! Will you die now, he wonders, or will it be later? He doesn't know, because I don't know, and it all depends on what you say next."

"We don't have money at the bank any more," says the man, closing his eyes as sweat makes them sting. "We're business advisors, mortgage lenders. No one has withdrawn cash from here in a decade."

"Hmm." Tortoisio looks thoughtful, and lifts the gun to scratch under his shell. "What year is it, then?"

"2172."

"I see." Tortoisio looks up at the little reptile sticking out of his head. "I think we have hibernated rather too long." The tortoise nods. Whether this is an affectation or not is hard to tell. Are tortoise and man simply one, or do both live in symbiosis?

"Let the women and children go, at least," says the man from the bank, heartened by not being dead. "Please."

Tortoisio scowls. "Yes, yes, whatever. This is clearly a

waste of everyone's time, and you have my utmost apologies. Run along kiddies, run along ladies. Sorry for the trouble!"

The women and children get up, and run to the door. There are tears from all sides, of relief, and despair, as families are divided.

Outside, the police welcome the women and children, wrap them in blankets, ask them for information.

Where are the Two Husbands? Will they even be needed? Be patient! They'll get here. Just keep reading to give them time!

"So tell me, my helpful banker," says Tortoisio, "how does a criminal go about acquiring money in this far-off future of yours?"

The banker tries to shrug, which makes him realise that the gun now rests between his shoulder blades.

"Embezzlement, perhaps?" says Tortoisio. "Precious metals. Copyright theft. Industrial espionage. I'm sure there are ways for a smart fellow like me to make a little money. But right now I am inspired to try a little bit of kidnapping for ransom. One must follow one's muse, mustn't one?"

The banker's breathing has become so shallow that he almost faints. His head hits the floor and it makes Tortoisio laugh. "Well, you've been very helpful. I shall let you leave the bank too, but you must tell the lawkeepers of this fair city of yours that I want fair recompense for my efforts today before I shall allow the rest of these men to leave the building. Do you understand?"

The banker is getting to his feet, dusting himself down, getting ready to run. "Yes. Yes!"

Tortoisio looks him in the eye and shakes his head. "I don't think you do." He points his gun at the unconscious security guard by the entrance. "Don't worry, he won't feel a thing."

Tortoisio pulls the trigger and the security guard erupts into a tower of brown paper that reaches the ceiling before coming to a halt.

"Never seen that one before," says the bank robber with a look of embarrassment. "But you get the idea. Get out there and tell them what I want. Money, valuables, whatever will buy me somewhere comfortable to live in a country with temperate weather."

The banker runs out, brown paper fluttering in his wake. On every sheet is an image of the security guard's face, a different expression on each one: fear, happiness, misery, hope, and so on.

"That leaves us," shouts Tortoisio. "I haven't even bothered to learn your names!"

There are eleven men left in the room, in addition to Tortoisio. What we haven't realised until now, and what Tortoisio still hasn't realised, is that at some point during the last fifty seconds that number went up from nine. The Two Husbands are on the scene!

They are at present crouching on the ground behind Tortoisio. They slid into the bank on a quantum pipestraw. A fake palm tree stands between them and him, but it won't hide them for a second if he turns around, and they are too far away to rush him - he would hear their footfalls, and even if they got him, he would have time to kill others.

If only they had landed closer. Husband One will have words with Husband Two about this later, and he lets him know as much with an angry toss of the head. Husband Two thinks Husband One should appreciate how much work went into creating the quantum pipestraw in the first place, and lets him know as much by sucking in his cheeks.

They have no weapons with them except their fists and their minds. No electronic or mechanical device would have survived the slide into the room. To be extra careful they were even wearing clothes that fastened with velcro rather than zips or buttons. Does that make sense to you? Perhaps not, but then you are not the genius engineer who created the quantum pipestraw, so no one would expect you to understand the intricacies of how it works.

Too far away for fists, so the battle must be fought with words. They stand up straight.

"Welcome to Pseudo City," says Husband One. "We are the Two Husbands. What can we do to make your stay here more comfortable?"

Tortoisio turns to face them, not in panic, but calmly, almost appreciatively, as if happy to face a new challenge.

"Good afternoon, gentlemen," he says. "How did you get in here?"

"A quantum pipestraw," says Husband Two. "I invented it."

"I'm sure you did. Good chap. And I appreciate your velcro fastenings. It makes me feel like I'm really in the future." Tortoisio points the gun in the direction of the Two Husbands. "Were you here in time to see what this does? That pile of paper over there used to be a man."

Husband Two clenches a fist and prepares to attack, but Husband One holds him back with a hand upon his chest.

"Though my name is Tortoisio, I'm not a monster," says the bank robber. "Like you, I have a job to do. My job is just to acquire wealth and power. Is that really so bad?"

"I've heard of you," says Husband One. "Before turning to crime, you were once a man of science. Professor Quigley, was it?"

"Quigg. Professor Quigg." He fires his gun at Husband One, who spirals hypnotically into nothingness.

While Tortoisio is distracted by the experience of watching Husband One disappear, Husband Two lets his fists fly at last. One hits Tortoisio in the face. The other hits the tortoise in the face.

No point in taking chances, he thinks.

He takes the gun from the unconscious criminal's hands and tells the hostages that it is safe to leave the bank.

"Get out of here," he shouts, "and send in the cops."

He looks at the gun, and looks at the spot where Husband One disappeared. Was he dead? After all their adventures, was this how it would end, at the hands of a bank robber with a tortoise buried in his head?

Husband Two lets out a shout so loud it makes the police pause for a moment before entering the building. Tortoisio is put into cuffs and hustled out of the bank.

"Whatever it takes, wherever I have to go," he vows, "I will bring you back. I promise. If I have to step into the very gates of hell itself and drag you out by the ears, that's what I will do. The story of the Two Husbands is not over. Not by a long shot. There are many more chapters to come, and I will not write them alone!"

He collects the sheets of the security guard, in case they will provide a clue, and walks back to the Husband Headquarters, his heart so heavy it could break his back.

Water Imperial

Charles Wilkinson

Early on the morning of the conference, the old manager's body was taken from his flat to the service lift and then to the back entrance to await the arrival of the mortuary van. John Cravis, the night porter, stayed behind to make sure this operation was accomplished before the cooks came in at daybreak.

By mid-day there were two men in the assistant manager's office, a high windowless room. A smell of damp paper and tobacco mingled with the dust and metallic tang of an open filing cabinet. Griffin Treginnis, the assistant manager, was seated behind the desk. In better light, it would have been possible to gain more than an impression of a white crumpled face with a few strands of hair falling across his forehead. The second man was standing: not so tall but compact, broad-shouldered and thick-necked, his stance suffused with latent power. From the one feeble light, placed so far above that its purpose seemed more to illuminate the ceiling than the action below, it was possible to make out his square head and skin pockmarked with white scars and purplish craters.

"As ever, Cravis, the Spa is greatly in your debt," said Tregennis. "I should go home now and get some rest."

"Will it be long before the new man arrives?"

"I shouldn't think so. We've already been in touch with the agency. Perhaps a glass before you go?"

"Thank you, sir."

A drinks cabinet in the corner contained a half-full

bottle of gin, but Tregennis moved a ruinous armchair away from the wall and crouched in front of a heavy iron safe. He turned a dial and opened the door to reveal a water fountain: a brass spout and a basin of stone surmounted by a carving of a head, possibly that of a beast or a wild-maned man. Tregennis filled two beakers with cloudy water, one of which he gave to Cravis, who took a grateful gulp.

In the assistant manager's office it was always twilight, except for one circle of light on the ceiling and the place where a yellow lamp illuminated the dust-swirl above the desk.

"Such horror and so early in the morning," said Treginnis, without a discernible note of feeling.

"If only they wouldn't exceed the terms of their appointment."

"Exactly. It is not given to everyone to comprehend the spirit in which the Spa is run. I'm sorry for the inconvenience, Cravis."

"Not at all, sir. I hope you don't mind my remarking that in the circumstances it was job well done. We were running short of the additive."

"Quite."

After the night porter finished his glass, Griffin made a phone call to A.T. Tregennis and Son, Funeral Directors, before resuming the many small duties that ensured the smooth running of the Imperial Spa Hotel and Conference Centre.

By eleven o'clock the hydrologists were arriving in their hundreds from as near as Cardiff and as far away as Canberra. Many favoured light-coloured clothes that reflected their professional preoccupations – shirts the shade of sky or storm-shadowed waters. A few opted for soft tweeds, grey-green and textured like lichen and cemetery moss. There was a Sikh with a

cumulous of a turban, a Chinese Canadian, a kilted
New Zealander and the first ever delegate from Tirana.
Briefcases and Gladstone bags contained papers on
hydrogeology, echohydrology, isotopes,
hydrometeorology and the intricacies of drainage
patterns, precipitation levels and predictions of flood
and droughts, along with schemes to build dams and
bridges and divert the course of rivers. Abstracts from
learned journals nestled next to underpants or under
sponge bags.

A woman with shoulder-length wavy hair, which
had kept the gloss of the sunlit day outside, walked
towards the table to register. Her pale skin had the
luminosity of a lady of the first Elizabethan court. She
had startling green eyes of a colour more usually found
a tropical paradise. If you looked very closely, you
would see she had been damaged by her purity.

Five minutes later, she pinned a badge with the
name Alice Swanne onto her summer dress. She
glanced around. Were there any other female
delegates? Her sex, it seemed, would yet again be very
much in the minority (best not to linger in the bar if
she wanted to avoid unwelcome advances veiled as an
interest in drainage patterns). Once again, she would
be spending far too much time alone in her bedroom.

Late in the evening, after the last of the council
workers and the caretakers had long since gone home,
the lights in the upper storey of a grey mansion in the
widest street in the town came on one by one, lights
which never shone during the day, not even when
dense cloud and driving rains shut out the sun.

After midnight, the night porter left the Imperial
Hotel and Spa Centre in the hands of his assistant and
made his way through the silent streets to the council
offices, which were in what was once one of the

grandest houses in the town. The rough sleepers had tucked themselves into their cardboard boxes, well away from the police and the outreach workers. Even the most habitual of the heavy drinkers had been wise enough to hurry back to the hostels and half way houses not long after last orders were called.

At this hour, John Cravis was accustomed to having the streets to himself. Apart from the rush of the distant traffic on the ring road, there was no sound except for the regular ring and echo of his footsteps on the pavement.

He was unsurprised to see every window in the top storey of the council offices lit up. The Convocation of Night was in session. The portico and awning at the main entrance suggested the architectural magnificence within, but during the day there was no doorman in top hat and tails to usher in the applicants for bus passes and petitioners for tax rebates and child benefits. He made his way along the street to a side entrance and rang a bell. There was not long to wait before the door was opened by a young man in a dark suit.

"Good evening, Mr Cravis. They say you're to go straight on up."

"Are they all there?"

"Yes."

Even after many years of presenting reports to the Convocation, Cravis could not suppress the tingle of fear that accompanied the exhilaration of knowing his opinions would be taken seriously by people of influence. As he stepped though the double latticed door and into the lift, he caught sight of himself in the mirror. His dark coat matched the menace of his shoulders.

The lift stopped and there was a wait – always just long enough to induce the dread of entrapment –

before the doors opened. Maurice Tregennis, Clerk to the Convocation, stood on the landing to greet him.

"Ah, John," he said, his lips stained with claret, "I thought I ought to let you know they'll want an update on the woman."

"Alice Swanne? We've not much on her. She is who she says is. Never been to the Spa before."

It was impossible to gauge the expression behind Maurice Tregennis's tinted glasses. Only once had Cravis seen him take them off: the eyes were tiny, almost unnaturally small.

"That may be so, but she's been taking an interest. There's no doubt about that."

"I'll make sure we keep an eye on her, Mr Maurice. To be honest with the complications arising from the death..."

"Exactly so... you've been fully stretched. But come through and take a glass before the meeting begins."

Maurice Treginnis raised his right arm in the direction of open double doors. The night porter saw a long wooden table on which rested a row of cut-glass goblets and several metal flasks. To one side, there was an enormous stone fireplace. The light from the burning logs flickered on the facets of an empty decanter, so that for a moment it appeared to have been filled with dancing fire. A servant with a second flask moved among the members of the Convocation. A low hum of conversation was punctuated by the spit and crackle of young wood burning. John Cravis put his hand into his inside jacket to check his report was still there and walked into the room.

Alice Swanne had dreamt as a surface hydrologist should: of the strange and variable pace of water; of estuaries, arroyos, oceans and the measurement flow of rivers. Her breathing was at its most peaceful when images of perfect irrigation systems and clear lakes and pools accompanied her through the night. At three, she'd awoken with a dry mouth and thoughts of drought and the over-pumping of aquifers.

Rising drowsily at half-past seven, she remembered having made an engagement, but not the details. They came back to her slowly as she brushed her teeth and banished the streams and wetlands to the back of her mind. An appointment with another delegate: she recalled his eyes, their green and black intensity, but not the rest of his face. They were to meet after the 10.00 am presentation on flash flooding. But what was his name?

He had approached her in the lounge after lunch. She had been about to dismiss him politely but firmly when he revealed he was a specialist in a branch of hydrology she'd never come across before. He could have information with the kind of explanatory power she had been seeking for over a year, since her symptoms first appeared.

When she entered the lounge, she did not spot him immediately. Only after a man waved from an improbable distance (the carpet stretched in all directions with occasional archipelagos of armchairs in the blue velvet vista) did she realise he was not late. He was wearing a white linen suit; his body looked about to disappear into the white leather sofa on which he sat.

He put out his hand and introduced himself as Aled Vank. His skin had the soft texture of the inside of a glove. "How was the flash flooding?"

"Good," she smiled as she put her bag on the floor and draped her scarf over a chair. "It was over very quickly and there were no victims."

"And you're speaking tomorrow."

"That's correct. An update of the paper I gave in Manitoba."

He sank back onto the sofa and looked up at her. Once again, she noticed the gleam in his black-green eyes. As she outlined the theme of her forthcoming lecture, he stared at her unblinkingly.

At the time, she registered his nondescript hair, mousy with a side parting, and his pale skin; though afterwards, when she ran through the scene, she found it was the eyes above the white suit that she could not forget.

"But tell me, where are you now?" she asked.

"I'm sorry?"

"Which university do you teach at?"

"I'm engaged in private research. The institute to which I am attached has no students."

"Ah yes, I remember you said you were doing some research into the significance of the wells hereabouts. Simply their curative properties, I hope."

"The springs in these hills were considered sacred before the arrival of Christianity. Some traces of these ancient convictions survive in remote areas."

He turned towards the window; the town lay huddled beneath them. The tallest building housed the council offices. In the distance, the colours of mountains and forests changed beneath sunlight and swiftly moving cloud.

"Have you noticed there are no churches in this town? Or chapels for that matter," he added.

"Unusual for Wales!"

"There were plans when the town expanded in Victorian times. But they came to nothing. Such were the restorative powers of the waters, the pump houses became the new churches."

"And so you're saying certain very old traditions were revived in a different, outwardly more respectable form?"

"That's true, but what is perhaps most interesting is that..."

"Go on."

"There are some wells in these parts that you will not find marked on any map."

And then she thought of a lake high in the mountains. Although the water was not frozen, in the blue-grey light its surface had the hard sheen of ice. The scene had the stillness of winter, but there were no trees to give an indication as to the time of year. Was this a memory of a place she visited, possibly as a child? She could not be sure. No wild fowl glided across the lake; not a reed whispered at it edge. On its inhospitable stony banks, sharp rocks and boulders had been piled up, either to protect the lake – or defend the surrounding countryside from whatever lay beneath its cold, smooth surface

---

"Her left breast was torn off, you say?"

"Yes, Dr Tregennis confirmed what the couple who found her told the sergeant. She was a local girl. There should be little difficulty in hushing the matter up."

The assistant manager, now revealed as a tall spidery man, his thin lips webbed with lines where the smile vanished, and Superintendent Alwyn Tregennis were walking down a long corridor towards a bar. The Imperial Spa Hotel was seven storeys high and surmounted by faux-medieval turrets. The facade, plastered with dark green stucco, resembled a merger between a Victorian button-manufacturer's Gothic folly and a guest house in an Alpine ski resort. So high-ceiling and ornate was the bar that it would not have been surprising to see an extravagantly coped priest raising the host in front it. Although it was late, well past one o'clock in the morning, there was a huddle of drinkers in the corner. Time would not be called until the Superintendent left.

"But you don't imagine there's any connection with...

the other matter?" asked Griffin. It had been a difficult day. A problem with one of the *sous* chefs. And now this: an inexplicable murder down by the lake.

"If there is a link, it's not at all obvious. Assuming we are correct about what it is Miss Swanne is looking for, I can't see how murdering a perfectly blameless girl, a promising soprano in the Choral Society, could possibly advance her cause in any way whatsoever."

"You think it has to be one of the people here at the conference."

"Well, it's not one of our boys, so it has to be?"

Griffin Treginnis's lips tightened, leaving a thin line that was almost indistinguishable from the creases around it. Underneath the bar was a metal flask containing the most fortifying of all fluids to be found in the Imperial Spa Hotel, but Cousin Alwyn would not approve of drinking it in public. Was the other flask, which he kept in his safe, sufficiently full to make it worth while suggesting they take a glass in the office?

"I'll give you a list of names. The conference has only two more days to run. Your lads will have to be pretty quick." Griffin signalled to the barman to re-fill the Superintendent's tankard. The flask was best reserved for later. "What do you make of the manner of it?"

"The killing?"

"Very violent. She'd been half-crushed to death before the mutilation."

"Sexual, would you say?"

"Possibly. We're waiting for the post-mortem."

"You haven't sent the body to..."

"No, of course not. Dr Tregennis is dealing with the matter. Down at the surgery."

After the Superintendent left, the bar emptied within ten minutes. Once Griffin had checked the night staff were on duty at the reception desk, he returned to his office and opened the safe. There was just enough in the flask for one full glass. It was fortunate he had not invited the Superintendent to join him. As he poured, he gave thanks for the fortification of water. He remembered by name the gods of the major and minor minerals. He praised zinc and copper, iodine, selenium and cobalt and, above all, iron. For it was through iron that the Tregennis family had lived in the hills since before the coming of the Celts; guardians of the chalybeate springs since the land that is now Wales was conjoined to the continent. He was of the most fortunate tribe, those with access to waters doubly enriched with iron. Yet as he drained the last drops he was uneasy. This murder spoke of practices older than the Tregennises' tenure. That there was a dark side to divinity, the urgent and necessary sacrifices, he was aware, but what occurred by the lake was truly terrible: a recrudescence of ancient disasters, calamities once believed to have died out, but now evidently alive, assumed to have been passed down from monster to monster.

When Alice was ten her sister drowned in the pool of a holiday villa her parents rented in Spain. It happened before breakfast. Waking in Spain with a warm wind in the curtains and the smell of the orange groves was wonderful until then – the moment she heard weeping in the garden and looked out of the window to see her mother, father and the maid grouped round a small figure lying near the edge of the pool.

It was a very warm and sunny day. A flawless blue sky stretched far above the baked ochre garden and its rocks, the gnarled olive trees and the headland that swooped down to the bay – its drawn bow of yellow beach and the eternal breath of its tides.

Of course, they all wanted to leave the villa as soon as possible, but there was an inquest to be attended and one day, just as she was coming down for breakfast, she stopped on the stairs and listened. Her parents were talking in low tones about "the release of the body".

After the accident, none of them could bring themselves to swim, but on the afternoon before they were due to fly home, she found herself alone by the pool and walking slowly round it, performing a ritual she did not understand. The intensity of the noonday heat had fled to a different time zone and the colours in the garden were a shade darker. The surface, a fretwork of knives and shadows, no longer hurt the eyes with reflected blade-flash. For a moment, she stopped and looked down through the patterned light to the bottom. At what point in underwater space had her sister stopped breathing? She would never know, but now she caught a sudden movement in the depths: a grey-brown shape with a snout-like protuberance. Just as she was about to focus on it properly it vanished into a corner, dissolving into the reflected foliage of an overhanging tree. It left only a curl of light on the surface like the flash of teeth. She knew at once what it was: an incarnation of an appetite that could only emerge from water. Of course, she had been far too young to formulate this discovery in words. Her first instinct was to flee to the villa, but she realised she would never be able to describe what had happened in a way her parents would understand. This threat she would confront alone. She started to walk round the pool in the opposite direction. After the second circuit, she began to count.

When she grew up, she devoted herself to quantifying the nature of water, gaining a complete mastery of its composition, and capabilities: the manner in which it falls from the sky, rises from the earth and flows across manifold surfaces; its ambiguous nature as a benefit that could be transmogrified to a hydra-headed threat (in the shape of storm, gale, flood, tide-havoc, deluge); she would comprehend its curative properties and role as a vector of disease; its potential to be transformed by magic. And she would spend her life as an adept of purity.

Day was not his element. While he was awake at breakfast, his last meal before retiring, it had been many years since he had seen the sun so high and bright. At least in the arboretum there was shade. John Cravis waited behind a Douglas fir, one of the many un-Welsh trees and ornamental shrubs planted in the parkland surrounding the pump rooms in the second half of the nineteenth century. He had a good view of the chalybeate spring. A local benefactor and former mayor had provided a bowl and marble stone with an inscription recording his own munificence. But it was the stone head, which could be that of beast, man or god, or possibly some combination of all three, on which visitors most frequently commented. Even John Cravis was only partially aware of what it represented, although he'd long ago detected the head's resemblance to the carving in Griffin Treginnis's safe.

He had been waiting patiently for over half an hour. One elderly couple walked over the wooden bridge before disappearing in the direction of the natural health centre.

Two boys, laughing as they played tig, skittered through the undergrowth and vanished into mature oaks and a stand of beech, all that remained of the original forest. He looked at his watch. What he could not dispel was the sense that someone was concealed in the woods. This person, whoever he or she was, had been waiting a long time.

And then Alice Swanne arrived. Cravis kept still, scarcely trusting himself to breathe. She had brought her own glass, which she put under the spout to catch the waters of the chalybeate spring. Formerly it was possible for all to take sulphur for heartburn, magnesium for tuberculosis; infusions of sulphur and salt; there was a lithia spring, the only one in Britain. Now there was only this spring, apart from the wells that remained unknown to the public.

Alice Swanne had drunk her glass of chalybeate water and was about to walk over the bridge to the lake. If Cravis didn't act soon, he risked losing her; yet some instinct told him to delay a little longer. He listened: the sound of Alice's footsteps on the bridge and then a movement in the bushes on the other side of the path. At that moment, he anticipated seeing a man or woman; what he did not expect was the slow emergence of a brown shape resolving itself into an animal he had never before encountered in Wales: a beaver, its fur sleek in the sunshine as if it had only just emerged from the water, blinked and bared its teeth.

The town rests on rock that was once the floor of an ancient ocean. As Griffin Tregennis walked through the corridors of the Imperial Spa Hotel, he was aware of moving over a space once occupied by seas but never navigated by man: the rock a composite of mud and the remains of creatures which swam in depths that vanished before the first human footprints marked the land.

The evening of the hydrologists' banquet. A renowned guest speaker was preparing to address the company, after they had drunk their fill of the finest mineral waters, sipped choice vintages and feasted on a five-course fish dinner. The bedrooms were likely to be empty. No one could hear Griffin's progress across the carpet, but even so he moved with the silence of silk being spun from a spider's abdomen.

When at last he reached Alice Swanne's room, he took out the master key and turned it in the lock. The room was so tidy that for a moment he thought she had left the hotel; then he saw her suitcase on top of the wardrobe. He worked swiftly and with assurance. There were some indications that the theory he put to the Convocation of Night was at least partially correct: a book on the sacred places of Wales, a map of the area, a bottle containing ferrous sulphate tablets in the bathroom. He replaced everything exactly as he found it.

As he made his back down the main staircase, laughter rose from the dining-room: the guest speaker was in gratifyingly good form. Soon there would be music and the sinuous dancing of the younger hydrologists. Tomorrow the delegates, some nursing hangovers that not even the precautionary pint of water before bed prevented, must go back to their universities, government departments and research institutes.

"Mr Tregennis, sir."

He had just come into the lobby and one of the receptionists, a young man distantly related to John Cravis, was trying to attract his attention.

"Yes."

"I thought I ought to let you know, sir. Miss Swanne, who was going to check out tomorrow, has booked herself in for another four nights."

"That's fine. We aren't busy."

"No, but you'd been asking..."

"You did absolutely the right thing to tell me. I want to be kept informed at all times. Miss Swanne is still at the banquet, I suppose?"

"Her key is in her pigeon hole."

"Good. Let me know if she decides to slip out..."

Water deep below the earth's crust is held in the mudstone rock for millions of years, where it absorbs chemicals from the rocks. The rainfall from above releases these ancient stores: wet seasons saturate, the table rises, replenishing springs. But Tregennis thought of wells, one not so far from where he was standing, fed by sources never known to the Romans and kept secret even from the Angles, Saxons and Jutes. In the town, there had long been wells – and the rumour of wells.

"I'm sorry. It's Aled, isn't?"

"Yes, me again."

Now she came to think of it, she had seen him – or someone very like him, hovering close by when she was having coffee with friends or queuing for a buffet lunch – a persistent peripheral presence. Yet she had been meaning to press him harder on his knowledge of the wells.

"Forgive me; I didn't quite catch what you were saying."

"I wondered whether you'd like to go up to the lake. There's a café and craft shop close by. If you don't mind riding pillion, we can be there within minutes."

Wearing a brown leather jacket and moleskin trousers, he looked more substantial than when she last saw him, although not as tall: stockier and with broad, sloping shoulders.

"Well, I'm not..."

Then she reminded herself that she must act soon. It was a fine day. She was confident the internal bleeding had stopped for the moment. The chalybeate waters were beneficial. And she could imagine a future beyond the ten months the doctors had promised her.

"Tomorrow perhaps?"

"No, now will be fine... if you can just give me five minutes to change into something more suitable."

While she put on a pair of jeans and a warm jacket, she tried to visualise his face and couldn't, apart from his black-green eyes – though even those were not quite as she remembered them.

Once on the back of his motorcycle, the wind cold on her face, her arms gripped tightly round his waist, she relished the rush of oxygen; for a moment she was the rightful inhabitant of her body – almost as she was before her illness.

And then they were sitting on the balcony of the café: their table with the red gingham cloth and teapot; a green lake tinted with sky and silver-veined with shifting light; the tarnished shadows of overhanging trees; ducks and swans paddling by the reeds; beyond the farther bank, wooded hills, the mountain ranges, the most distant an indistinct smoky blue. A small island in the middle and, as if swimming away from it, a water sculpture: a crypto-Nessie for kids with an arc of foam spouting from its mouth.

"Is the monster connected to some local legend?" she asked. "Or a borrowing from north of the border."

"Very much the latter, in my opinion. Welsh monsters do not always announce themselves as such straight away."

"Inconvenient to have a stream of water eternally issuing from one's mouth."

"Just so. But how often does anyone take into consideration the monster's point of view?"

In a guide book, bought before coming to the conference, she'd read how in Victorian times the lake had been used for regattas and recreational sailing. A domesticated stretch of water, she would have said, if she hadn't known that a few years previously an algae had turned it toxic. The problem had been dealt with, but no one was fishing or punting.

"Apparently this lake was poisonous until fairly recently."

"I know. But as you can see, it's fine now. The wildlife is back."

She was glad she had come out. The woods on the far bank were soft greens and browns, young delicate trees and ferns out of which it was difficult to imagine anything dark and disreputable crawling. For the last two nights she had dreamt of the lake she saw in her waking vision. Now she had this pleasant scene with its jolly monster to set against her nightmares.

"Last time we met, Mr..." She had forgotten his surname.

"Vank."

"I haven't come across that name."

"It's not that common."

"Is it Eastern European?"

"Not at all. It's a very old Welsh name – possibly even pre-Welsh."

"Like the traditions attached to the wells you were going to tell about."

"Was I?"

"You said there were certain wells in the town that are... in private hands. Wells not known to the general public. How did you to come to be aware this?"

"The Vanks are an old family. It is information of a kind we've always had. Now I hope you don't mind answering one of my questions."

"No."

"What is your interest in the wells? In strictly hydrological terms how remarkable do you expect to find them?"

"It's the water itself that is of interest. I've heard it comes from one of the deepest sources in the country. The minerals it has absorbed may be of great benefit to me."

"There is always," Aled replied, speaking softly, "a

danger when we use what has been drawn up from below. And yet it is probably not the water in itself that presents the greatest hazard; it is the way it is being treated."

A fine day for a visit to the undertaker's. John Cravis reached the quiet side street in which A.T. Tregennis and Son, Funeral Directors, had their premises a minute before he was due. The façade had recently been painted and the company's name glittered in gold capitals on a dark background. In the front window, there was a display of funerary objects, white marble on a purple cloth.

As Cravis opened the front door, a bell rang.

"Ah, Mr Cravis," said a gangling, sandy-haired man in late middle age, "come to collect the flasks, have we?"

"Yes, Mr Tregennis, if they're ready."

"All waiting for you in the fridge. The full eight pints this time – and more."

"The Spa will be much obliged, I'm sure."

"Not too much spilt during the incident, I'm glad to say. I'll send down for them now."

Nine flasks come up from the basement, the one in which the last drips were stored lighter than the others. As if they were merely milk bottles, Cravis whistled cheerfully as he loaded them into a metal container.

"Mr Griffin says to expect another gentleman caller by the middle of next month, sir."

"The new manager not settling in well?"

"They never do."

"Thank you, Cravis. Tell him I'll make sure a space is available."

Right on time, the dark blue limousine with tinted windows (the Spa reserved its use for discreet errands) drew up outside. Mr Glyn Tregennis opened the door and looked up and down the street before nodding to Cravis.

"Afternoon, Mr Cravis," said the driver as the night porter took the back seat and draped a tartan rug over his burden. "Not your usual hour."

"No. But if one has to be up and about it's good to have such clear weather in which to go about one's business."

The car smelt of luxury, leather and cigars. It was always a privilege, Cravis thought, to be in the presence of its walnut dashboard and to be able to observe the shoppers without them looking in.

"Round the back, Mr Cravis?"

"That would be wise."

Once John Cravis had deposited the flasks filled with the old manager's blood in the fridge, he walked through the kitchen, the dining-room, the cocktail bar and into the lobby. A list of the morning lectures had been pinned to a freestanding board positioned to one side of the reception desk. The assistant manager's door was ajar and Cravis stepped through.

"Ah John. Everything in good order, I trust?"

"Completed according to your instructions, sir."

"Good. Close the door behind you."

Griffin Tregennis took off his glasses and rubbed his eyes before leaning back in his chair. An internal report lay open on his desk.

"It's about this business of a local girl who was found up by the lake. One of Dai Hedges's daughters, as a matter of fact. You know the family?"

"Yes, sir."

"Very loyal to the Spa. Always have been. And they're quite prepared to let Superintendent Tregennis conduct the investigation as he sees fit. Which is just as well."

"Oh?"

"It's definitely not somebody in the town – and we've run a check on everyone staying here and thrown up nothing suspicious. It's the mutilation, see. Very showy. This sort of thing gets repeated and attracts all sorts of attention. The kind we don't want."

Only the desk light was on. Now the door was closed the corners of the room were no longer visible. For a second, it was as if they were in a much larger space, a plain on which a creature with singular appetites roamed in inscrutable darkness.

"I'm not sure what to suggest, sir."

"Don't worry, I'm not asking you to suggest anything. But pay attention. Just about the one piece of solid evidence the Superintendent's men have uncovered is this. Miss Hedges was seen by the lake a few days before the... event. And she was with someone. A man. Now what is curious is that she was sitting in his lap and singing to him. The sort of song you might sing to a troubled child or, if I can remember how the witness phrased it, *someone who was in great agony of mind.*"

It was the last day of the conference, but Alice Swanne had neglected to attend a single lecture. Outside, mist rose like smoke from the woods; an escarpment was blurred by cloud. She had been alone in her room with her laptop. Aled Vank was a man who existed without having left a digital trace. It was true he had never claimed to be a member of faculty at a university or college, but he had no publications to his credit and she could not find a mention of an article he had written or even the abstract of a paper presented by him. But he had done no more than claim to be engaged in "private research". What did it matter that he had not appeared in print when he was informed on the one subject of interest to her? She glanced at her watch.

Once again, Vank was sitting on the white sofa in the hotel lounge. This time his clothes, the colour of earth, were immediately visible against the pale background. His legs were shorter than she recalled; indeed, like a child's, they barely touched the carpet. His shoes were small and polished to a fluid gleam. As he smiled, she noticed his prominent teeth.

"I've been thinking about what you told me," she said, once the coffee had been served. "None of these wells is known to the public?"

"That's not quite true. Families that have lived in the town for generations know of their existence but not their location. And they've learnt it's best not to inquire."

"And the hazards?"

"Very considerable."

"What can possibly be so dangerous about wells fed by natural springs? I understand these sites were once sacred. I've heard the myths about the eels that are said to guard them. But surely..."

"There are no eels. The wells are not in themselves dangerous. It's the fortification of the waters, the attendant processes of additional mineralisation and the customs connected with it that are..."

"Yes?"

"Both necessary to ensure the special properties of the water but also the cause of secrecy."

"I'm not quite sure what you mean."

"Let's say certain ceremonial actions are performed that are not entirely legal. But I'll take you to one of the wells – if you are sure that is what you want. You should be aware we may encounter... some opposition."

She explained she had no option. Whatever was killing her could not be overcome by conventional medicine. She could only postpone her death with a diet of iron and the mineral waters of the chalybeate springs. Soon these treatments would not be enough.

"Some nights," she told him, "I dream I am dying of purity. And then I wake up and find that it is so."

"A strange gentleman has just checked in, sir," said a young receptionist.

Cravis's nephew or cousin? Griffin Tregennis could never remember which. A fine blustery day outside, with the light running off the mountains. The young man stood by the door, reluctant to enter the dark and dust of the assistant manager's office.

"In what way strange? We get all sorts here, you know. You'll have to get used to that."

"Well, he... I just thought I ought to..."

"Come in and explain yourself clearly."

"He didn't have any luggage."

"And?"

"He appeared to be slightly damp... well, more than damp... wet."

"That's not unusual in Wales, lad."

"But it hasn't been raining. Not since yesterday morning."

"What is his name, this man?"

"That's what I was coming to. He hadn't booked and so I asked him to fill in his details and gave him a key. But then the phone rang. When I turned back he was gone, but what was really odd was there nothing on the form, except for a few pale blue blotches. And yet I could have sworn I saw him writing."

"And so you don't know his name?"

"No."

"I think perhaps we had better check on this guest of yours. I suppose you can remember the room number."

"Yes, sir. Forty-nine."

Griffin Tregennis took the spare key off its hook and within minutes they were stepping out of the lift and on to the first floor landing. Now the conference was over, few of the rooms were occupied. All that could be heard was the distant sigh of the doors closing and their footsteps, faint on the carpet.

Three sharp knocks on the door and no reply. Treginnis knocked again, louder. And then from inside the room: a noise like something large slapping water. The two men glanced at each other and the assistant manager turned the key. The bedroom was empty, but beyond they saw the bathroom door open slowly. Steam curled into the room, followed by an arm covered in wet red-brown fur – and then a head with the eyes of a crocodile.

She was half asleep in her room. Hypnagogic dreams of the ways to control water accompanied her towards tea-time: visions of aqueducts, levees and canals. As she turned over, the white waves of the sheets rose. She thought of the sovereignty of the sea over the earth; how water prevails over everything but emptiness. The dams will crumble; the dykes be riddled with holes.

No one had ever slept in her bed; she had never given herself to another. Once she was proud of her purity; now she understood what it had cost her. Day by day her blood thinned; she was becoming closer to water, closer to dissolution.

Her room overlooked the hotel's back garden, once one of the finest in Wales, but the weather had turned the grass dark and sodden; the paths were slippery with yellow and pale gold leaves. In the distance, mist rose from the lake. Aled Vank had told her his home was not far. There was no doubt he loved her. He'd asked her to come to his lodge: a simple place. But if she went, would she end up staying the night? She knew he would not take her to drink at the well without making his own demands: a price to pay for the pact.

It was almost two months since her last appointment with her doctor, the day when they'd reviewed the results of the tests.

"And so none of you have any idea what's wrong with me?" Months of appointments, blood tests, examinations and scans and she had nothing to add to the initial diagnosis. "Apart from the fact that I'm mysteriously losing blood."

"I'm sorry; this does sometimes happen. A patient becomes anaemic, and there seems to be no obvious explanation. The assumption is you are suffering from internal bleeding, but I'm afraid we've been unable find the cause. All we can suggest is that you keep taking the iron tablets. They'll help to slow the rate of your decline..."

"So I'm slowly dying? Iron tablets – that's all you can suggest."

The doctor took off his glasses and began to polish them with a handkerchief.

"This is off the record. But I was discussing your case with a haematologist. Not one of the local chaps, but someone I was at medical school with. He tells me that there is this place in Wales..."

And now she was here with the rain falling. Beyond the garden and the lake, the mountains were merging with the clouds. She knew that water was colourless in small quantities; with every day that passed her blood became less vivid. The world was seventy per cent sea. Her body in its natural state was more than half water. She was so tired the last heat of her flesh would turn to mist.

The phone rang, ending the death reverie:

"Yes?"

"It's Aled. A slight change of plan. I think I mentioned my lodge is prone to flooding. It would be easier if we met at the hotel and then we could go on to a place I know."

"Where are you now?"

"At the hotel."

"Give me half an hour an hour to freshen up. "

"I'll be in the lounge."

Fair and foul are near of kin and fair needs foul, I cried. Who was that? The Irish poet. She walked over to the sink, turned on the cold tap and let the wintry water flow over her wrists.

"You're sure it was a beaver..."

"I told you. A beaver with the head of a crocodile."

None of the sounds in the rest of the hotel reached the assistant manager's office. Griffin Treginnis was seated at the desk; his hand holding the telephone was yellow in the lamplight.

Silence on the line, and then: "You know what this means?"

"Of course," said Griffin.

"I'd no idea the levels in the lake had risen so high."

"You sure that's how it escaped?"

"How else could it have got out? I mean no-one could possibly want to help it escape!"

"Maybe, Maurice. But what are we going to do about it? I mean it just walked in here and calmly checked itself into one of the rooms. That's never happened before."

In the assistant manager's office, you could not hear the guests at reception, the cool jazz playing in the newly refurbished cocktail lounge, the clatter of cutlery in the kitchen or the hum of conversation in the dining-room; even the movement of the lift as it rose from the ground floor was no more than a faint vibration.

"No, it hasn't. Well, not in our lifetimes."

"Cravis can't cope. We must call the police."

"Does the new manager know about this?"

"No."

"Where is he?"

"With what's left of the old manager. Waiting to be decanted."

There was his voice – and the voice at the end of the line and the lamp shining on the top of the desk. No sound from outside. For a moment, it was as if everything were about to vanish into the darkness and silence.

"Where's the creature now?"

"I'm not sure. As soon I saw it, I locked the door and went to find Cravis. Now he's claiming there's no sound coming from there."

"We'll need chains."

The monster was in the lounge drinking a cup of coffee. No one could see how its fur was wet or its head that of crocodile; the centuries of longing were not visible on its placid, unmemorable features. It was wearing a white suit, which in certain lights was a very pale blue. At least it was not in the lake. But it wished there was a newspaper that expressed its point of view.

A waiter was coming towards it but the monster could tell from his deferential expression there was nothing to fear.

"More coffee, sir?"

"Please, but for two. I am expecting a lady to join me."

What are the appetites of a monster? Her skin was divine pink rose and milk and would be soft on his tongue. He imagined them together naked, his crocodile eyes on her flesh; his teeth waiting to feed on an angel.

And here she was coming through the door. He slipped the photograph back into the inside of his pocket and stood up.

Her hand in his, both so smooth. He knew his touch would feel gentle on her skin, through the years of living underwater. Some centuries he hardly stirred from the depths of his immemorial habitat, for the act of rising was also the risk of being alone with his desires amongst rocks, stones and reflected sky.

"I'm sorry to hear about your house."

"It's fine now. I may have exaggerated the extent of the problem."

"And so?"

"I think we'll visit my place first after all; then later we'll go on to one of the wells. It will be easier if we leave it until after dark."

The murderers would be looking for him soon. He had hoped to adopt a more leisurely mode of seduction, a drink and a meal first; no one understands the importance of normality's mask more than a monster.

It was not quite dark when an elderly couple out for a walk saw a motorbike driven at great speed down one of the roads that leads out of the town. As the driver leant into the bend, his passenger, a woman who was not wearing a helmet, fastened her arms tightly around his waist. The vehicle straightened but instead of continuing down the highway, the motorcyclist, who had every appearance of being in charge of his vehicle, drove straight into the lake.

For a moment, the couple stood still. There were no boats out on the lake and the ducks and swans had retreated into reeds. Rain clouds gathered on the horizon. The wooden sea serpent, forever frozen in the act of moving forward, contemplated its arc of falling water. There were no lights on in the restaurant, which closed at four o'clock once the season was over. The old man half-expected the motorcycle to surface by the artificial island in the middle of the lake.

As a pensioner of the guardians of the wells, she lives on fortified water. The moment of her freedom was the instant of her capture. She has a small room on the top storey of the hotel. The mirror reminds her how one kiss almost ate her face away. There will be many days to think of the immortality of her lover, who, once more alone in the lake high in the mountains, nurses his longings, while time shifts cloud and sun over the rippling surface which is the roof of his home. His enemies have placed stone upon stone around the shore, but she knows he believes in the triumph of rain, storm, the melting of glaciers, the floods that will raise the level and liberate him once more.

They have told her what happened. Maurice was the first to see the avanc on the island: running through the trees, form-switching from man to beaver, from beaver to man; Griffin said how he heard her singing: though the words were faint, he could just make out the melody; John Cravis was the first to smell her blood. In his joy, the avanc half crushed her, but soon the men were on the shore, their chains ready. She recalls nothing, not even Aled's kiss, his crocodile grin coruscating in the dark. (And later the hand of Dr Treginnis on her pulse.) Or how the storm passed and the moon came out to shine on her first lover, bound and glittering in his chains.

Some days she thinks of the derangement of drainage patterns; the imprint of streams on a delta like the lines on the devil's hand; the confluence that creates floods. And at nights she dreams a history of drowning.

Twice a week, a key turns in the lock and Griffin Tregennis enters with a glass of pink fortified water. If she lives long enough, he informs her, she will forget her wounds; it will be as if her face is without blemish: "No one should be allowed to think of themselves as permanently damaged."

She studies the statistics of rainfall. We are mostly water, she tells herself, and must be sustained by water, even its impurities. Our complicity is unending. There is comfort in the analysis of inches.

They come to her at night: Griffin, Alwyn and the others. Even John Cravis. They bring her the truths of *bodily lowliness*. Was that how the poet expressed it? She tries not to think of her debt: how she came to be in her comfortable room with its view. Yet she knows it's the murderers who saved her from the monster.

Author's note: *An afanc, addanc or avanc is a lake-dwelling creature from Welsh mythology. It is mentioned in The Mabinogion. The Irish poet whose verse is quoted by Alice Swanne is W.B. Yeats.*

The Assassin's Lair

A Dim Star Is Born, Part 2

Howard Phillips

The would-be assassin was nowhere to be seen. I shrugged off the attentions of the corridor's bizarre atmosphere and strode steadily on. Weird faces loomed at the corner of my eyes – no doubt my imagination, or an optical illusion. How far I walked cannot be said – a mile, or a metre? I don't know. But at last, the entrance long out of sight, I came to a second door. A trap door.

Was this literally a "trap" door, I asked myself? The possibility could not be discounted. I had many enemies. Fewer that still lived, admittedly. (I have tried to remember from where I stole that line; if you know, get in touch and I will amend future publications of this story to give proper credit.) I have thwarted much evil in my life. I have irked many good people. It was entirely possible that traps had been laid for me.

And yet... How could they have known that I would be in that street? (They could have been watching, waiting for the right moment!) How could they have known that I would be so attracted to that photograph? (A scientific analysis of my romantic preferences!) How could they have known that I would enter the mysterious doorway? (Anyone who's read a novel of mine would have known that!)

Sod it, I thought. It's not as if I have anything left to live for.

I opened the trap door and jumped down. The shout went up.

I was in the centre of a medium-sized control room. Larger than NASA's, smaller than the BBC's. All about me men and women ripped off headsets and threw them to their desks, grabbing whatever implements were available that might usefully be applied to my person. At a glance, I estimated that there were ten or twenty assailants. Once they were lying unconscious on the floor I was able to take a more precise count: seventeen, nine women, eight men, their nationalities unknown, their ethnicities various. Some had the jagged teeth of my friend, but not all.

I had intended to save at least one of them for interrogation, but by the time I reached the last one, a five foot tall Indian woman who aimed numbing knuckle-punches at my biceps, I was barely thinking, a battle robot without an off switch, a mechanical man with the instincts of a mongoose, a fighter in a frenzy of foe-tumbling! I was in the zone, and if I had taken it easy on her who knows who might have been creeping up behind me. So I let her have the old one-two to the noggin and laid her gently down to sleep with her colleagues.

"Drat!" said I upon realising my mistake. I do make them every now and again. Or at least I try to, to make myself more likeable. "Who will spill their secrets to me now!?"

I looked to the equipment which they had been using. Computers, monitors, great screens across the walls. Maps with marked locations, pinned pictures of their quarry, Twitter searches. The writing on the computer screen was in a language I did not understand – not a surprise, since I speak few languages these days. What's the point when people think you're wiser if silent?

But those Twitter searches were useful, because they

were searching for variations on a name: Pierre Silver Samuel. What a daft name for such a gorgeous man. But what's the point of being beautiful if you don't take advantage of being able to get people to take a silly name seriously?

The Twitter searches brought up nothing of note. This was a man who lived largely offline. There were tweets here and there that might possibly be referring to him, but no Twitter account of his own, no mentions, no retweets.

I had to find him. To protect him, of course – what did you think? That Howard Phillips would be such a slave to a pretty face that he would battle a room of maniacs and scour all of London? Well, okay, that too.

The other monitors might be more useful in that regard. I looked at the locations circled on the maps, studied the photographs. I knew some of those places. *The Haunted Quill*, *The Signed and Clothbound*, *The King's Pamphlet* – these pubs were all places where one might find that terrible breed, those wolves among humanity, the strippers of verbiage, the festering wounds of the literary world.

Poets.

It would seem that Pierre Samuel was a poet. Like me. Perhaps we knew some of the same people, moved in the same circles, patronised the same Arts Council-funded publishers. But we had never met. If we had, I would have remembered. My life would have changed course – in his direction! – so much sooner.

For all my adventures in music, and the galaxy beyond, my heart was still in poetry, and I had never lost touch with the lyricists of my youth. Frank Tank, the man who never wore sleeves when there was a couplet to be declaimed! Sonia Bubonic, fiercest rhymesmith in all of Europe! Hades Corpus, who claimed to be ten years dead, and had himself wheeled onstage in his coffin, that he might pass judgment on the living from his miserable resting place!

I hadn't lost touch, but it had been a while since I saw them in person, a while since I went to those pubs, took part in those poetry slams, pulled my moleskine notebook from my back pocket. There was a reason for that. The conclusion of the last adventure in the Saturation Point saga (*We Slept Through the Apocalypse*) had forced me into some unwelcome realisations about my poetry. I had stopped writing it, stopped performing it; I had even thrown away my rhyming dictionary. It was for the good of the world.

But I hadn't left the scene. I could still appreciate the poetry of others. I was, in fact, the administrator of the English Poetry Prize, a position I had originally taken on with no little dismay that it would prevent me ever winning the prize for myself, but some happiness that I would now have a good excuse for not doing so. That gave me an idea. I took out my notebook and wrote it down.

By that point groans and croaks were beginning to rise up from the floor around me, so I took out my phone, snapped as many photographs of everything and everyone as I could, and began to smash things with a crowbar one unfortunate had attempted to use upon me. I had no idea which panel would open the exit, so I walloped it all in hope of getting something right.

Half the room was in ruins before I hit the jackpot, and a chain reaction of tiny explosions began to run across the consoles as yet untouched by my warlike ways.

"You fool!" came from behind me. It was the man whose gunslinging on Regent Street had started all this. So he did speak English! "You don't know what you've done!"

"Maybe not," I replied, "but I know I enjoyed doing it. And that's not bad for a Tuesday."

His head tipped back in horror, eyes wide and mouth poised to shout, and I looked behind me to see the control room collapsing. "Get out!" I yelled to my former foes as I jumped up to climb through the trapdoor and out of the room, but few were conscious and as I pelted down the twisting corridor I assumed none would survive.

It's a hard life being a villain. And often a harder death.

In the distance I saw the door opening out onto Regent Street, then swinging closed, then opening again. My efforts in the control room had been at least partly successful, then. Now I just had to get there before the corridor collapsed around me. Whatever this place was, it was dying. Whatever had sustained it was gone. Whoever it served would want revenge. Meh.

My feet burned and grumbled as I hammered them upon the floor, pushing me on as my swinging arms dragged me along. The shifting, shimmering fractals on the wall tried to distract me but I wasn't having any of it. I ran and ran until the exit was an arm's length away.

And then the door closed again.

"Oh, blimey," I said to myself. "Best of luck, Howard."

I turned to see how long I had left. Not long at all. Barely fifty metres of the corridor remained, and even that looked frail. Worse yet, my friend with the teeth was running in my direction, a new pistol in his hand. As yet the twisting of the corridor had prevented him drawing a line upon me, but as he got closer that protection would vanish.

Any chance the collapsing corridor would swallow him before he was in range? No. He raised his gun.

I raised an eyebrow and began to laugh at the silliness of it. Howard Phillips, poet, musician, artist, novelist, lover and philosopher, to die here, unknown, by an unknown hand, defending an unknown man who would never know the sacrifice I had made on his behalf. I prepared for death in the only way I knew how: I let a single tear drop down my cheek and whistled the opening bars of Mogwai's "year 2000 non-complaint cardia". Sing along at home if you know the one I mean.

Then: what! The door behind me opened, and I jumped back, pulling it shut behind me even as bullets smashed into it on the other side. A narrow escape!

A millimetre away from closing it completely, I stopped. That would condemn my assailant to death. Was that fair? I didn't know much about him. They hadn't asked me to invade their base and destroy it! What if I was wrong about them?

I left it ajar and ran away.

You may judge from what follows whether I was right to do so.

Whale on a Tilt

Andrea M. Pawley

"I know about your scoring, Brun," Leteesha Prime says.

She's loud, too, like she wants everyone around the conference table to hear, but I don't care if the other judges find out how I score *Tour Groups Battle!* teams. I'm not breaking any Corporation rules there. It's my gambling that can get me kicked off the judges' panel. I won't give up gambling for anything. More money to bet on drone fights was half the reason my brother and I started our own Tour Group, *Eighteen Holes and Counting*, long ago. The other half was the formidable Mordata Mordunn.

"Did someone buy you off?" Leteesha says. Out the window behind her, flight traffic pauses at a sonic barrier on the Las Vegas Strip. Five years ago, Leteesha was the first heavy metal flautist to sell a hundred million song tracks, but she has no idea how to maximise profits on *Tour Groups Battle!*, the most-watched game show in the world. News of an affair between us would boost both our revenue streams. The second time she refused my advances, I pointed out her shimmer suit's green haze meant the device was struggling to hide her cellulite. That wasn't exactly true, but my brother was the one with the manners, not me.

"I hear the Osbourne Institute is enhancing musical talent at a genetic level," I say to Leteesha. "The world's going to pass you by if you don't take advantage of every opportunity you're given."

Leteesha's eyes narrow at me. If my brother were around, he'd call me an ass. I'd call *him* a moron for getting eaten by a crocodile on the back nine.

Heads around the conference table tilt in our direction. Bickering among the judges is normal before the Battle meeting. Afterward, it's a race to see who can get the largest payouts from the news feeds by dishing on what happened. It's all profit. Everyone gets a cut, so I don't mind the game.

I offer Leteesha a million-dollar smile at fourteen per cent interest.

"It isn't all rules and judging, Teeshie." I say. I know she hates her nicknames. Mordunn is the only one who could have given Leteesha access to my private scoring history, which means the boss has noticed me. This bodes well for my future income with the Battle Corporation. "You need to ride the wave, Little Teesh. Find your sondo-froc."

But I don't think Leteesha can. The flautist's shoulders quiver whenever she's near a microphone. Last month, Amy Vu's House of Coins took my bet that Leteesha won't make it a year as a judge.

Leteesha's cheeks redden.

"Aren't you the least bit bothered by what you do?" the jittery flautist says. "Marking low scores for the clear winners in each category is wrong."

"What an interesting accusation. But how would you know how I score? That's confidential information."

Leteesha's shimmer suit darkens.

"You just seem like the type," she says.

"There's only one champion in this game." I tap Mordata Mordunn's pendant on my lapel. I touch it low so as not to cover her ice-blue eyes or smudge the perfect sparkle of her close-cropped white hair.

"How do you know she wants to be the only champion?" Leteesha says.

"I'm surprised bagpipe school left you so naïve," I say.

Leteesha's shimmer suit chills to blue. Somewhere above the conference table, a microphone opens up. Every muscle in my body tenses.

A voice screeching through speakers says, "Mordata Mordunn!"

The boss's lean hologram image appears at the centre of the table and rotates in place. She's mesmerizing or terrifying depending on your point of view. She's wearing a skin-tight black leather bodysuit, my favourite. She stares without blinking. Mainlined nico-coffee couldn't have twitched her features.

Mordunn had once been captain of *Casinos Across America,* the only Tour Group to ever score above ninety per cent. They were the greatest team ever, and she was the greatest captain. Leading a tour group requires a blunt ruthlessness I admire. *Casinos Across America* wasn't indestructible though. A few weeks after they won that long-ago season, all five *Casinos* members came down with a mutant strain of Legionnaire's Disease. Only Mordunn lived. Soon after, she was in charge of *Tour Groups Battle!* and the underlying Battle Corporation. She hasn't granted an in-person interview, germ-laden or otherwise, since taking over. Under Mordunn, at least twenty-eight per cent of the qualifying world population watches each episode of *Tour Groups Battle!* Last night, when *Four Days in Rome* and their vicious money belts pushed past the binocular-wearing *Team Bird,* the viewer share topped forty-one per cent.

I try to look Mordunn in her hologram eyes, but her steel-blue glare threatens to scythe me in half. My gaze falls to the glittering trail of rings on her right hand, the one famed for dominating the slot machines. Over and over, I've demonstrated my loyalty to Mordata Mordunn by helping ensure no team ever scores higher than *Casinos Across America*. The Chief Battle Officer may not have asked me for this favour, but she must understand my gift to her legacy. Better placement at the judges' table isn't too much to ask in return. I could be near the centre where advertising revenue is better, not on the fringes where I only get offers to peddle the third-best-selling stim-fizz, but Mordunn's assistants refuse to respond to my requests for a private holo meeting.

"Viewership is sagging," Mordunn says in a voice like diamonds cutting silk. Her holo-form stalks the judges' table.

I force my gaze to rise to her well-muscled shoulder.

She says, "I've instituted changes that will necessitate your immediate action."

The other judges around the table shift in their chairs. I take a deep breath. I've loved Mordunn since I was a boy. She's a perfect being, unbeaten and unbeatable. I modelled my own captaincy of *Eighteen Holes and Counting* on her.

"The public wants more influence on the final scores," Mordunn says. "Beginning next season, I'm increasing the public share of the vote to fifty per cent. I'll retain twenty per cent for myself, and the judges will get thirty per cent."

Stunned silence envelops the room. Each judge's share of the overall vote has always been five per cent. Between the ten judges, we control fifty per cent of the score. I'm not worried about the scoring change though. I've been so good to Mordunn. I'm sure she'll look out for me.

Chester Fwinstat blurts out, "You can't do that. Our advertising revenue will be affected."

Mordunn's gaze slices into Fwinstat.

"Next season, *Tour Groups Battle!* will only have

three judges," Mordunn says. "Each will contribute ten per cent to the final vote, thus *increasing* their potential advertising revenue. Seven of you will not return after today's championship Battle."

This is what I've been working toward. Ten per cent of the vote will double my revenue. I dare to glimpse at Mordunn's perfect chin.

"Leteesha Prime, Upapu Gwembo, Yvegeny Petron," Mordunn says. "You'll be returning next season."

Protests erupt around the table, but not from me. I'm elated to be staying on as a judge, and I'm not surprised.

Above the noise, Mordunn says, "At the conclusion of the today's episode, per Battle Clause Sixty-Six, you will each have ten seconds to say farewell to the viewers. Any overages will be added to your required advertising payout at the contractually-agreed rate."

I skin a smile at the other judges. I'm going to make a fortune alongside Leteesha, Upapu and Yvegeny. I'll pay off a few debts. I'll visit the new track in Provo where horses with grafted-on wings are starting to race. That's money ripe for the taking. I look around the silent room, but something isn't right. A few of the other judges seem to be shouting. I can't hear them. For a moment, the world goes fuzzy. I think back to what Mordunn said. Three judges would be staying on. Not one of them was me.

I can't swallow. I try to cough. I reach for a glass of water. It's too small for me to drown in, but maybe I can find a window to jump out of. Better to die that way. Amy Vu is the most savoury of the characters to whom I owe sums with more zeroes than I have fingers. Noise like ball lightning explodes in my ears.

"For the rest of you, Battle Clause Sixty-Four is instituted," Mordunn says. "The Corporation requires your advertising payouts in five days."

Chester Fwinstat rises from the table. His pulsing neck inflates his face.

"Are you saying we owe *you* money for our advertising contracts?" Chester says.

In my tunnel vision, Chester see-saws between the room's ceiling and the floor.

"If you care to dispute your legally-binding commitment," Mordunn says, "you can speak with the Battle Corporation's lawyers, but don't expect any sympathy from me."

The coins rolling through my gambling fantasies fuse into linked discs flaying my body. I don't have enough money to cover my current gambling debts much less to pay the Battle Corporation the advertising revenue I anticipated and already spent. My heart pounds in my chest. I push myself to standing, though I can't feel my legs. I glare at the hologram face of that bitch Mordunn.

"Have you seen my voting record?" I was yelling.

The Chief Battle Officer's terrifying gaze lands on my sweat-soaked form.

She says, "Your low scoring is part of the problem, Brun." Red sparks flare in the depths of her ice-blue eyes. "And while you're the kind of chump I love to see across the poker table from me, your gambling violates Battle Clause Seven. Be sure to clean out your Battle Quarters before the finale." Her gaze swivels to the other suckers. "That goes for all of you."

I hurl my drinking glass at the boss. Water splatters across the table. Neither Mordunn's image nor her expression flickers, but the projectile has the decency to hit Yvegeny Petron in the chest.

I throw back the last of the Glenlivet from my Battle Quarters liquor cabinet. This sixth shot feels the best.

"It's a bad bet, Brun," Amy Vu says in my display.

"That's only happened once in the show's history, which is why the Thu-Dice no longer allow locations that contain both wild dogs *and* cheetahs."

"But you agree there's a chance no one will win the Battle today," I say.

She sighs. "There's a one in sixty-four million six hundred seventy two thousand four hundred eleven chance. So yes, there's a chance, but not much of one for a man who's lost seventeen of the last twenty bets he's placed with me."

"You're the worst bookie I ever met."

"I'm not a bookie. I'm a businesswoman and a friend."

"If you aren't going to take my bet, I can find someone who will." I try to be firm, but my words slur.

Amy's expression hardens. "After this, you pay me what you owe me."

Her fingers dance over an interface that sucks away the funds I'd earned two hours before by violating Battle Clause Two and giving the news feeds an exclusive about the shake-up in judging and the new scoring rules. Amy cuts the link. After I win this bet, Battle Corporation penalties won't matter.

I swallow a green greeter pill I found under the Glenlivet and leave everything in my Battle Quarters in at least two pieces. I take the lift to the judges' balcony above the arena and the audience. The double lenses of Scotch and a hallucinogen paint all the straight lines in waves. I sit down at the judges' table. Blood drips from a cut on Chester Fwinstat's forehead, which suggests mine isn't the only altered Battle Quarters. The make-up bots swarm him. I knock mine aside. The show starts.

"Welcome to the season finale of *Tour Groups Battle!*," the announcer's voice booms inside the arena and out to the rest of the planet. I've never met him, but I assume he's a bastard. "*Four Days in Rome* meets

Machu Picchu Ruins. The Thu-dice have given neither team a location advantage. We turn to the Bay of Fundy where only one Tour Group will emerge as this season's champion!"

My plan is to stop that and win my latest bet, but my head is fuzzy from the drugs and the alcohol.

Images of the two remaining teams appear at separate ends of the holo-stage. *Four Days in Rome* stands with arms linked like small-town tourists on a crowded sidewalk. In broken Spanish, *Machu Picchu Ruins* chants their request for directions to the bathroom. Credit chits float down onto the arena audience. The crowd goes wild. I scan the space near the judge's table for items that will fit into my pockets. I palm a *Tour Groups Battle!* fingerpen near Leteesha's hand. As if Mordunn knew this would be a time of thievery, all other moveable objects seem to be attached to the judges and the nearby Battle technicians.

The holo-stage shows water pushing into the Bay of Fundy. *Four Days in Rome*, the team closest to the bay's mouth, will have to deal with the rising water more quickly than *Machu Picchu Ruins*, which is hunkered down near a boat tilted atop the mud. From the shore, fishermen in a diner look up from their coffees at the unexpected figures on the mud flats. Water from the incoming tide crests the soles of *Four Days in Rome*'s walking shoes. The team changes into open-toed sandals. Beside me, Leteesha searches for her fingerpen. I try to remember why I stole it.

Two kilometres away from *Four Days in Rome*, *Machu Picchu Ruins* scours the Nova Scotian landscape for stones to fit the altar they're unpacking. For *Machu Picchu Ruins*, the tidal bore's approach is minutes away. A *Picchu* member lays down on the altar. Another player raises a small object that looks to me like a skinny cow in gaudy earrings. The rest of the team begins to chant.

I lean forward. My chair tilts with me. I squint at the monitors and controls near the judges' table. I remember Mordunn fired me from the show. Worse, she called me a chump. I realise what I'm sitting on isn't attached to the floor. Standing, I turn and grasp the chair by its base. The chanting from *Machu Picchu Ruins* grows louder. I heft my siege weapon and tense to run toward the Battle controls.

Leteesha says, "What are you—"

Light flashes across the top of the holo-stage. The crowd gasps. I hesitate, which is easier and less wobbly than the thought of running. The Battle technicians bend toward their monitors. *Machu Picchu Ruins* looks up at the sky and forgets to chant. *Four Days in Rome* pauses, too. A gust of wind sweeps the Bay of Fundy. In a blur, tag-out sashes are ripped from all ten *Tour Groups Battle!* team members. Audio in the arena crackles with feedback from an unused communication channel opening up. Another light flash explodes across the sky. Halfway between the judges' table and the Battle controls, I put my chair down.

"We have come to play," a voice says. I can't tell if it's male or female.

Cameras pan upward from the Nova Scotian flats to the sky. A thin, winged vehicle as long as a city block hovers in the air. The craft's skin pulses with soft green light.

"We are travellers, too," the voice says.

The craft's image vanishes. Instead, an orange cylinder appears on the holo-stage and unrolls into a wafer-thin figure that tries to look human. I assume the image is compliments of the green greeter I took earlier, but I'm not sure. I glance at the other judges. In a first, shock unifies everyone at the table.

"Bring forth your champion team," the orange figure says. Its mouth moves out of sync with its words. "And we will Battle."

Some of the arena audience scuffle to leave. It occurs to me I just won the bet about no team winning the Battle. My luck is turning. I sit back down in my chair. I wish I'd bet more.

From the judges' table, Leteesha shouts, "You can't just come into the game at the championship round."

The orange holo-image says, "We have already done this. Our team is *Chwzpr No Mleev*." Four other figures shaded lighter than their leader unroll in the holo's background. The new aliens bulge with conviction in all the right places.

"Your team isn't allowed to play." Leteesha trembles like a plucked igil. "The rules say you have to wait until next season."

"How can we prove our qualifications?"

"You may be qualified to play, just not right now. You'll have to compete at the beginning when the new season starts."

An orange figure materializes in front of Leteesha. The centre of the alien's plane bulges toward the flautist. Leteesha turns away, but she's not fast enough. A wave of heat washes through the room. Where Leteesha had stood, only dissipating smoke remains. As a judge, Leteesha *had not* lasted a year. That's two bets in a row I've won.

"That magistrate has been overruled," the leader of *Chwzpr No Mleev* says. "One of our own crew will judge instead."

The orange figure who'd eliminated the flautist slides into her chair.

The alien leader says, "Any other objections?"

I shake my head in a manner designed not to draw vaporization attention. So do the other judges.

Chwzpr No Mleev's leader says, "Bring forth your champion team."

The orange judge in Leteesha's chair bulges a face out of the plane of its head and nods with abandon. I'm glad I've already moved my chair away.

Yelling, a lone voice in the arena crowd says, "You've tagged them all out!"

"Not those teams," the alien says. "Your true champion team."

The crowd begins to murmur. Electricity rides the air. A name is shouted. The chanting starts.

"Mor-dunn!"

"We no longer Battle," Mordunn says. Her voice booms through the arena's audio.

"Then you are not champions," the alien says.

He must have a death wish. The holo-image in the arena splits, and Mordunn appears beside *Chwzpr No Mleev*.

"My team is no more," Mordunn says and doesn't kill him with a look.

The crowd is silent.

"Interesting," the alien says. It moves with its team away from the display. Multi-coloured gesticulations follow. Something flashes red on the monitors near the judges' table. A technician gasps. I look. The monitor shows over fifty per cent of the world viewing audience is watching. That's a new record. The number climbs.

The leader of *Chwzpr No Mleev* turns again toward the camera and says, "Single combat then."

Mordunn's reply is immediate. "Agreed."

At the centre of the arena, the Thu-dice megahedron appears and rolls. Images from locations around the world flash across the holo-stage with each upturned Thu-face. Despite the odds, Las Vegas lands Thu-side up. Mordunn would have seen to that. The arena erupts in cheers.

"This is a lucky break for Mordata Mordunn," the *Tour Groups Battle!* announcer says. "It's her strongest setting and the city that holds the Battle Corporation headquarters. Fans of the untested *Chwzpr No Mleev* can only hope their own champion has a gambling streak." Cameras adjust to the new Battle location. Referees deploy. The announcer's voice drops to a whisper. "Some say the reclusive Chief Battle Officer hasn't come into physical contact with another person in five years. How will she handle interaction with an alien culture?"

A moment later, Mordunn appears inside the Hyper-Luxor Casino. Its pyramid walls pulse with catolights. Gone is Mordunn's leather bodysuit. She's wearing a garish Hawaiian t-shirt and a red tag-out sash. Heirloom casino coins poke out from between the digits of her left hand. Her right is free for the slots. A green-visored hat shields her eyes from the glare of gambling den lights.

Inside the Olde Excalibur Hotel, *Chwzpr No Mleev's* champion materialises. Goth princesses and emo knights flow past the too-thin alien wearing a *Tour Groups Battle!* tag-out sash. One hotel away, Mordunn takes off at a run toward the designated Battle location. Crowds of Hyper-Luxor gamblers part. Palm trees flutter in Mordunn's wake. She stops to scan coins into a row of ancient one-armed bandits. She pulls the lever. Sevens slot into place.

"Jackpot!" Mordunn says. Her jewelled fist pumps the air. She sprints away to the electronic cling-ding of funds falling through the World Revenue Service and into her bank account.

Comments from the local crowd bubble through the simulcast.

"Wasn't that Mordata Mordunn?"

"What about the Bay of Fundy?"

"Are we on *Tour Groups Battle!*?"

Mordunn bursts out of the casino and onto Las Vegas Boulevard. She sprints toward the Battle Treasure Chest and claims the prizes inside. The arena audience cheers Mordunn's good fortune. *Chwzpr No Mleev* is not yet in Mordunn's sight.

Above the din, the *Tour Groups Battle!* announcer says, "For opening the Battle Treasure Chest, Earth's champion is the proud owner of five thousand of Opie's Best Marbles, a can of Cleaner Spaces Aero-Hydro Sanitizer and a pair of Nitroxium Air Skates." Another cheer bursts from the crowds. Nitroxium Air Skates are all the rage.

Approaching quickly, *Chwzpr No Mleev's* champion appears a block away from Mordunn.

"The two champions have spotted each other," the announcer says. "It looks like there won't be any sneaking around to snatch tag-out sashes or set complicated traps. This confrontation is going to be face-to-face!"

Three levels of Boulevard traffic stop around the designated Battle location. Jubilant carplane horns trumpet encouragement. Mordunn empties the sanitizer tube in her opponent's direction. The skates mould themselves onto the Chief Battle Officer's shoes and gel around her ankles. Fewer than thirty metres separate the contestants.

"Your talents are wasted on this pathetic excuse for a biome," *Chwzpr No Mleev's* champion says. "You are a hero. Come with us, and you can spread your teachings throughout the galaxy. On Vlorgk Zup, you will be worshipped for the champion you are."

"Stop your talking," Mordunn says, her tag-out sash streaming, "and face your single combat!" Mordunn takes off toward the alien. Rising half a metre above the ground to the maximum height of the air skates, she heaves the open bag of marbles at the orange figure. The alien wavers. Sensing victory, the crowd screams. *Chwzpr No Mleev's* champion thins. It grows longer and wider. It spreads backward over transports, people and the potted foliage floating in the centre of the Boulevard. The alien plunges toward the Mordata Mordunn event horizon.

"Big money!" Mordunn says. She coasts onto the alien's flattened form and hurtles toward her opponent's tag-out sash. Too fast for the skates, the orange blanket lifts into the sky. Mordunn's arms shoot out and pinwheel. Casino coins go flying. The alien-as-blanket ripples. Mordunn tumbles into its folds. The world's crowds gasp. The Chief Battle Officer slashes with her stone and metal jewellery at the massive orange creature. The alien wraps itself around Earth's champion.

From somewhere inside the blanket, Mordunn screams, "Cheaters!"

The Chief Battle Officer and her kidnapper rise high into the air. Cargo bay doors open on *Chwzpr No Mleev's* spaceship. The package carrying Mordunn disappears inside. The holo-stage audience is silent, but most of the judges begin to cheer. The orange magistrate vanishes. The alien spaceship disappears from view. I always knew being filthy rich would feel this good. I reach over to my display and enter my first-ever perfect score for *Chwzpr No Mleev*.

Cybertronica

Les aventures fantastiques de Beatrice et Veronique

Antonella Coriander

Bzrk909 realised it was over. No longer forced into that gross physical form, she was back in her natural state. The cyberweb. No up, no down, no left or right, just a whirl of information, colour and light. She was character data in a world of infinite data, no longer perched behind artificial eyes. Here, all could be known, exchanged and absorbed, the only limit her needs and desires.

She reflected upon her self-representative visualisation, the way others would see her here. She was instinctively wearing her favourite skin, a three-tiered arrangement of spinning trapezoids, and saw no reason to change it. The cyberweb blew refreshingly through her gaps. Trillions of datalings swirled around her every corner, and she luxuriated in their presence.

//Back home. Gosub transit,// she thought to herself.

=Wait!= came a message from a nearby webnoid. //Don't leave me here.//

//Describe yourself,// sent Bzrk909. She had no time for this. She was scheduled to report.

=It's me, Veronique. What's happened to us?=

Bzrk909 stopped to perform a new iteration. //Veronique? This designation is unfamiliar.//

=Beatrice, I know it's you out there. Help, please! I'm desperate.=

The communication seemed unstable. Bzrk909 wondered if the system had contracted a virus. She shouldn't hang around. There was work to be done. She couldn't sort out the problems with every program she encountered. She kept moving. Unfortunately, there was a queue to get onto the fibre, giving the fault time to importune her further.

=You can't leave me like like this, Beatrice! I don't understand what's happened to us!= For a fraction of a second there were no further communications. Then: =No, wait. Not Beatrice. That was never your real name, was it? Bzrk909, is that it? Were you always this, whatever it is? Was I, and I just didn't know it?=

Whatever this fault was, it seemed to know enough about her activities to cause trouble. She had on occasion used the designation Beatrice, when it was necessary to take action in the slow world. These matters were supposed to remain secret. Had she been Beatrice this most recent time? She wasn't sure. Either way, she didn't want this fault blurting out her business to every passing subroutine with time to listen. Bzrk909 stepped out of the fibre queue and approached the webnoid.

//My designation is Bzrk909. Please refer to me as such. What help do you require?// she asked.

=Get me out of here!=

Bzrk909 had never heard a message broadcast so widely. Programs all about turned to see what was happening. She glowed red with mortification – until she deleted the softapp that had betrayed her so. She silenced all in/out communications, waited till attention had gone elsewhere. It didn't take long. In this place data moved quickly, and there was always new data to be considered.

//Be quiet,// she sent at last, //or you will stay where

you are till deleted. Do you wish to acknowledge receipt of this message?//

At first there was no reply. Perhaps the program was considering its options. If so, it soon realised it had just one. =I do acknowledge receipt of this message.=

//Good. I will try to get you out of the webnoid. Please be patient.//

=Thanks.=

It was a complex problem that would require a complex solution. The sentience, whatever form she took, was firmly embedded in the webnoid. Like a column of numbers scattered through a spreadsheet. It would be hard to get her out.

//How did you get in there?// asked Brzk909.

=I don't know,= replied the sentience that had designated itself Veronique. =Last I knew I was on a flying bowl, and there was this weird girl called Cornelia Gilligan, and she said she was going to switch off our robot bodies. Don't you remember any of this?=

Brzk909 twirled her middle trapezoid. //It is... not familiar. However. You seem to have been embedded within this webnoid for an extremely long time. There may have been time for my memories of these events to degrade. I will need to consult my backups.//

=What?= there was clear panic in the communication. =Goodness me. How long?=

//>30,000,000 fractions, at least,// sent Brzk909.

=What is a fraction? That doesn't mean anything to me.=

//Then there was no point sending you that figure. Please hold your communications for now. I must concentrate.//

It took a great deal of careful work, taking much more time than Brzk909 could rationally account for. There was no reason for her to expend so much time upon this fault. She had more important work. And yet she felt it necessary. She scanned her components for clues as to why. If any knew anything, they weren't responding. It was often that way after time in a slowsuit. It took time for her routines to get back up to normal speed.

Eventually it was done.

The troublesome sentience slid from the webnoid. She seemed unsure of herself, emerging quickly but reluctant to release the connection completely.

//Refresh!// ordered Brzk909.

=Don't rush me!= sent the Veronique. =I'm not used to this.= She settled into a pool of viscous data. =This doesn't feel right. Can you help?=

//Extrude a connection,// sent Brzk909.

The sentience did, and Brzk909 torrented a set of relevant subroutines to it. //Helpful? Or not?//

=I think so. Give me a second.=

//A second?// Brzk909 just had to verify the data. //An entire second? I am willing to assist. Not devote my functional lifetime to your cause.//

=Okay, okay, it's just a figure of speech. Or sending, I guess. I think I've got it. How does this look?= The Veronique resolved herself into a rough caricature of a human form. =Ring any bells?=

Brzk909 had met humans recently. Not this one, so far as she remembered. //I'm afraid not. Perhaps your resolution is too low. Come with me. I have work to complete, and those to whom I report may be able to help you further. And on the way we shall access my backups, and see if my archived memories hold any information regarding you. Is that acceptable?//

The humanoid nodded.

//Please send information directly rather than modifying your skin. I may not always be scanning you.//

=Understood. Thank you, Beatrice. I mean Brzk909.

Whatever your designation, I knew I could rely on you.=

//Try not to attract attention.//

They got into the queue for the fibre. Veronique would have done anything to avoid attracting attention. It was hard – she was clearly providing these entities with new information. Just how long had she waited for this opportunity? Only the malfunction Brzk909 seemed to think she was would blow a chance craved so long. It seemed to her that she had fallen asleep on the flying breakfast bowl and then woken up in that webnoid, but she believed the assurances of Brzk909. If it had been an instant transition, how would she have been able to perform any of the actions since her contact with the former Beatrice? She must have had time to adjust, acclimate. Perhaps her consciousness had dropped into the first webnoid it came to, and since then she had drowsed, not fully conscious, until Beatrice once again came through the same entrance to this place.

Or maybe it was Beatrice who was getting it wrong. Could Beatrice have been fooled into thinking this was all normal?

For her part, Brzk909 was as puzzled by her interfaces with this Veronique. Even as she loaded herself onto the fibre, she wondered whether she was malfunctioning. This was not her mission. This was delaying her mission. There would be consequences.

//CEASE DATA ENTRY!// sent an unfamiliar program. Brzk909 could not identify the source of the message, and so chose to regard it as addressed elsewhere.

//Get on!// she sent to Veronique, as subtly as she could. The peculiar fault still hesitated, so Brzk909 expanded for a fraction and dragged her inside. She released her hold instantly, and would have reddened again had she not already deleted the relevant subroutine. They hurtled at the speed of light in the direction of Brzk909's data store. Their positions relative to each other did not change, allowing them to exchange data as they travelled.

=What's happening?= asked Veronique. =Who was shouting at us like that?=

//Shouting?// Brzk909 accessed her memories of the slow world to make sense of the word. //Oh, you mean capping? System monitor, probably. You stand out here, Veronique. I don't know if you're a human who's become a program, or a program who thinks she's a human, but other programs will want to find out. And they won't mind if your system integrity fails during the investigation, so long as your data is intact.//

=So you saved me?=

//Probably. But we don't know. It's possible she was talking to someone else, as I chose to pretend. Possibly she was curious about you, but not enough to create a system-wide alarm. Let's hope not or we shall have to run new iterations after reaching my backups. There's something we should fix before we upload to my place. May I tinker with your data?// Veronique assented, so Brzk909 extended herself again, more gently this time, to engage with Veronique. //How does that feel?//

//Pretty much the same,// sent Veronique.

//Good. As I hoped. But you will stand out a little less now. Any chance you could abandon the humanoid form for something more geometric?//

Veronique shrugged. //I could try. It's nice to be back in one piece. The robot body I was just in... it took a lot of damage.//

//I understand,// sent Brzk909. //You have an attachment to that form. Well. Other programs *do* wear humanoid skins. They aren't exactly in fashion. But you might be able to get away with it. I won't press the matter if it contributes to your stability.//

//Thanks. Where is it we're going? How long will it take to reach your backups?//

Brzk909 scanned their cyberweb surroundings. //My data store is in one of the most prestigious parts of the cyberweb. I say this not with pride. I say it to prepare you for its grandeur. We are mere fractions away. Prepare to disembark.//

Veronique glowed a funny colour. //Erm... I'm not sure how, Beatrice.//

//My designation is Brzk909! When will you process that information? Is your processor malfunctioning?// Veronique's visualisation shrank to half its previous size. Brzk909 struggled to regain her composure, and finally managed it. //Apologies, Veronique. I must myself process how strange this is to you. Grasp this and I will lead you off at the appropriate moment.//

She narrowcasted a data strand for Veronique to hold.

It was every bit as incredible as Brzk909 had led Veronique to believe. Immense towers of light glittered as far as she could scan, each glitter a datum, each tower a digital life.

Veronique expressed her amazement with a flutter of yellow blips around her skin's head. She meant for them to look like tweety birds in an old cartoon. It looked more like she was affecting a halo. Not that Brzk909 was scanning her.

//It's amazing,// sent Veronique. //I've never...//

Brzk909 was not happy. //No. It's not right.//

//What's wrong?//

//Data towers are missing. *My* data tower is missing.//

Though Veronique understood little of the cybernet, she knew that could not be good. //Has it been deleted or something?//

No communications passed between them for a fraction. Then Brzk909 sent back: //Impossible. That would be an illegal operation.//

//An illegal operation?//

//It could could irreparably harm the system's integrity. It's not just about me and my history. Think of all the hyperrefs and interlinks to my data? All now rotten.//

Brzk909 computed quickly. It would take an immense amount of power to do this. No single individual program could have wiped her backup. Not without the approval of the system administrators.

The admin back at the fibreway. Brzk909 had assumed she was after Veronique. Time to recalculate. Could the admin have been there for her?

//What have I done?// she sent, in low resolution. //They wouldn't be coming for me like this, taking such terrible risks with the data structures, unless I was guilty of the most terrible crimes.//

//Wait,// sent Veronique, //don't panic. I know a thing or two about crime, and that isn't you. You're a straight arrow. A good girl. A police officer. You coudn't be a criminal if you tried. You'd arrest yourself before that happened!//

Brzk909 was grateful for the sentiment. //I hope you are right. That's how I visualize myself. Problem is, before a spell in the slow world we have to partition ourselves, due to the low capacity of the slowsuits we wear out there. I don't know what I left behind. I might have deliberately deleted all record of my crimes.//

She scanned the data towers that remained, and had an idea. It was a dangerous, rather reckless idea.

Could it work? Was it possible?

//I have an idea,// she sent to Veronique. //Neighbouring data towers inevitably end up mirroring each other's data, especially at the top where there is spare capacity. If we could get up there, perhaps we could find reflections of my most recent activities.//

//Sounds good,// sent Veronique, her visualization glowing an enthusiastic green. //How do we do it?//

Brzk909 led her to the foot of a tower. This former neighbour of her tower was devoted to the data of Faben-Dah-237a, a tenth-level defragmenter.

//We're going to have to run,// sent Brzk909. //Run up the side of it.//

//Won't that damage its data? When we cross over it?//

//A little,// responded Brzk909. //Those of us in the data security services are given this ability for emergencies. Try to follow my line, so that the damage is limited.//

//No need to recalculate, that sounds good to me.// Veronique was having fun, for the first time since waking up in this place. //This is an illegal operation too, though?//

The edges of Brzk909's trapezoids drooped a little. //Yes, I'm afraid so. I wouldn't be doing this if there were any other option. If we set off a data cascade, it could cause untold system-wide damage.//

Veronique clapped her visualised hands together with glee. //Let's do it, then! It's not a party without some danger!//

Brzk909 extended a data pack to Veronique, who installed it without question. //You will now be able to activate sticky mode. This will let you climb the data tower. Note however that the stickiness may leave some residue on both sides.//

//You mean I might leave some of my data behind?//

//And you might pick some up. If you find yourself increasingly preoccupied by matters of defragmentation, let me know.//

//Will do. And good luck, Brzk909. As Beatrice you were a good friend to me. Even if you did let me get half-eaten by a crystal dinosaur. I want to be a good friend to you if I can. It will be a novel experience.//

The two of them had barely reorientated themselves in the right direction, ready to ascend the data tower, when the fibreway exit behind them exploded with activity. A dozen system administrators, blue by nature, now flashing orange! And their data sniffers, each pulling at its leash like a rocket tied to a tree!

//Time to go!// sent Brzk909.

She led the way up the tower, moving as quickly as she could. Where possible, she scanned the data ahead, trying to avoid overrunning the information that might have deep personal significance for this defragmenter, Faben-Dah-237a. Her days at defragmentation college (well known as the best party school in the entire cybernet!). The production of her derivative systems, and their subsequent development into fully functional programs. Her memories of art, theatre, music – for all these things are present in the cybernet, though not as you or I might understand them. Brzk909 aimed for the tedious days of work, the days when nothing went wrong, that were indistinguishable from all the others.

However, as she ascended the tower and accrued that data, Brzk909 learnt to appreciate the joys of a perfectly performed defragmentation: interrelated data recombined and gathered together in tidy patterns; the drive space opened up for new use; the increased system speed that resulted. She began to wonder how long it had been since *her* last defrag.

At least that kept her mind off their pursuers.

//You have to stop!// barked one of them. //This is a violation of data security protocols! Stop or we will stop you!//

Brzk909 knew that they would hesitate to do so.

Unless they could actually lay their data streams upon her, any measures they could take to stop her – for example a remote buffer deletion, an explosive data extraction, or shots from the stream interrupters held in their hands – risked doing infinitely more damage to the data tower than she and Veronique were doing by climbing it. They would keep up the pursuit, and only take more desperate measures if the two runners were about to escape or escalate.

That was no reason to be overconfident, though. They were barely a quarter of the way up the tower and she was already tiring. The sticky data dragged at her, and it took a force of will to keep pushing on. And while she thought she could probably outrun the system administrators, and Veronique definitely could (especially if she didn't need to restrain herself to Brzk909's pace), those data sniffers were fast – and off their leashes! They were closing the information gap rapidly and would soon be sinking their data hooks into her programming!

//Veronique!// she sent back to her new friend. //When I flash the signal, take the lead!//

//Don't do anything stupid!// sent Veronique.

//I wish I didn't have to!// replied Brzk909.

She began to lead the chase in a slow spiral around the data tower, rather than running straight up. That meant slower progress, but it also meant the pursuers furthest back would be partially unsighted by the curve of the tower. She did it gradually, so that the system administrators would keep chasing her, rather than realising they would be able to catch her more quickly if *they* took a straight line up the tower.

Once they were spread out, and the system administrators wouldn't necessarily be able to see the foremost data sniffers, Brzk909 began to look out for what she needed. Bad memories. The worst moments of Faben-Dah-237a's life. Something she wouldn't mind doing without.

At first the pickings were slim. Faben-Dah-237a had lived a pleasant, uneventful life in the cybernet. There was an accidental data loss here, a failed defragmentation there. Nothing that would do any damage.

Wait, there it was, up ahead, to the left!

One of Faben-Dah-237a's derivative systems had contracted a virus, a very bad one. It had ravaged the poor little thing, pushing her data integrity to its very limit, and Faben-Dah-237a had not been sure whether her derivative would survive. Scanning ahead, Brzk909 was relieved to learn that the derivative had survived the episode, and had gone on to great things in the anti-virus department, helping many others to survive.

But Brzk909 didn't want the happy ending, just the disaster. She scooped up the memory on the run, and edited out the bits she didn't need, leaving only the pain, suffering, fear and misery. It wasn't quite there, so she added a new ending: the derivative's system integrity failed, its originator left desolated. Satisfied, she made two dozen copies.

Veronique could see what she was doing. //Darn, Bea. Good job you aren't evil, because you're way too good at being bad!//

//Don't be offended if I take that as an insult!// sent Brzk909 with a smiley. //Are you ready?//

//I was ready the day I popped out of my webnoid!//

Brzk909 gave her the signal, then turned to stand her ground as Veronique dashed past.

Now she wasn't moving, the snarling sniffers closed the gap on Brzk909 almost instantly. As the first leapt at her, its glistening hooks lining a maw that stretched wide enough to engulf her upper trapezoid, she sent it a copy of the bad memory.

Normally, it would have had no effect. The sniffer

would have rejected it as random data passing by, but not now. Just like Brzk909 and Veronique, the sniffer had been crawling up the side of Faben-Dah-237a's data tower, absorbing her thoughts, memories, identity. And so the less than intelligent sniffer recognised the infoscent of the bad memory; it was one of its own memories, to be absorbed and processed without question.

A fraction of a fraction later the sniffer was curled up and rolling back down the tower, wracked with all the pain, suffering and misery Faben-Dah-237a had felt, and a good deal more that she hadn't.

If the other pursuers saw the sniffer fall, they didn't know why it fell, and they kept coming. One by one Brzk909 took them out, with a ruthlessness that surprised herself. She didn't even know that she was in the right – should she not have handed herself over to them, rather than fighting? The answer had to be no: even if these system administrators and their sniffers were innocent of wrongdoing, they must be in service of whoever had deleted her data tower, and if she didn't bring that person to justice, these programs would eventually suffer just as she had done. This was hurting them, but it was for their own good.

The sniffers had all fallen, and now came the system administrators. They knew to be careful, and didn't come straight at her, spreading out in an arc to divide her attention.

//You have to stop!// sent one. Brzk909 recognised her, now that she was so close. Hod-23-zoop. They had worked together. Solved cases together. Absorbed media together in the evening. //Brzk909. Trust me. We have to take you in. Don't make it worse!//

//I'm sorry,// sent Brzk909. //I really am. But something is rotten in the state of the cybernet, and I have to figure it out.//

She sent the bad memory at Hod-23-zoop, and then

at each of the other pursuing system administrators. They doubled up in agony, broadcasting the most terrible screams.

Brzk909 turned to follow Veronique up the tower.

The system administrators would only be temporarily incapacitated by the bad memory. Though affected by the same accretion of Faben-Dah-237a's memories as the sniffers, they were much more intelligent and would know the bad memory wasn't theirs, however hard it hit them at first. Brzk909 had to make the most of this temporary advantage, and so she put everything she had into climbing as quickly as she could – while still doing her best to avoid damaging Faben-Dah-237a's data tower.

She was up to the top third now, and scanning she discerned Veronique up ahead. She still didn't understand the connection she had with this strange program, but it seemed she could be relied upon. She sent ahead, asking Veronique to wait for her.

//Are they all gone?// queried Veronique after they were reunited.

//The sniffers are,// replied Brzk909. //The admins will struggle for a while, but they'll soon be after us again, more determined that ever. And I can't pull the same trick twice – they'll be ready for it. They might even reciprocate. The admins see the worst of the cybernet – if they send those memories at us we'll wish we'd never started this.//

//So why aren't we still running?//

Brzk909 led her around the data tower in a horizontal plane. //Because we're here. My tower used to stand just there.// A trapezoid elongated towards a conspicuous gap among the data towers that surrounded this one. //Look down at these. These can't be the memories of a tenth-level defragmenter.

She would never have visited the slow world. These are my memories, mirrored by this tower.//

Veronique scanned the information upon which they stood. She saw the ocean, roiling and roaring during a lightning storm. Human hands holding a bicycle's handles. She saw herself, far below, unconscious of the threat from the sea below and the storm above.

//That's me!// she sent excitedly. //Don't you remember any of that?//

//I do not,// sent Brzk909. //It seems to confirm what you've been saying, but there's nothing here to explain the deletion of my data tower. We should move on.//

They began to climb the tower once again, and as they climbed the reflected memories became more recent. Veronique saw a beach lined by trees. She saw herself again, lying on the beach. Despite their hurry, she scanned back over her shoulder to see if there was anything to explain how they had arrived on the beach, after the bicycles were hit by lightning. Nothing. Either Beatrice had been unconscious too, or those particular memories had not been mirrored.

Veronique was not the kind of person to be particularly fretful about the past. The future was the thing! There was always a new caper to plan! But she did like a puzzle, and it frustrated her that this mystery was still unsolved.

//This is all very hard to credit,// sent Brzk909, as they passed the memories of the dinosaur battle (Veronique chose not to scan that one too closely) and their first encounter with Cornelia Gilligan.

//As it was at the time,// replied Veronique. //And imagine how weird this place is for me. I was born in what you call the slow world.//

Brzk909 scanned her carefully. //Or you think you were. As I have recently demonstrated, memories can be reproduced, edited, falsified. Your body was as robotic as mine, and here you are in the cybernet, an artifical intelligence. Does it not seem likely that you are, like me, a digital native, sent out into the slow world with altered memories?//

Veronique shook her visualisation's head. //Logically, that makes sense. But I don't feel it in my heart.//

Brzk909 tipped her upper trapezoid. //What heart?//

They kept moving upwards. Far, far below, the administrators were recovering. There was no longer any point in hurrying, though. Either they would find the information they needed, or they wouldn't. Moving quickly up the data tower now would only increase the chances of missing an essential datum, especially as the reflected memories became sparser and more difficult to spot amidst the bulk of Faben-Dah-237a's information.

Brzk909 was developing a real affection for the defragmenter. The program had performed her essential duties with dedication, with little thanks other than the satisfaction of switching on each day to see the cyberweb running smoothly. She had undertaken post-graduate research, and developed new formulae for the restructuring of data. That growing affection made Brzk909 feel all the guiltier about interfering with her data tower like this. It wasn't just the damage she had done herself – she doubted that the pursuers had been as careful as to where they trampled.

Veronique recognised further memories as they climbed. //Here's where we fought the giant crystal pilot fish, and here's the battle through the base. Remember this bit, where we found a crate of apple crumbles in a storeroom, and started throwing them at the crystal cuboids? We had no other weapons, and at least the apple crumble obscured their vision a bit.//

//No, I don't,// sent Brzk909. //We need to move past this to reach the memories neither of us have. How did our adventure together conclude? What's the last thing you remember before waking in the webnoid?//

//We were in a flying breakfast bowl with Cornelia Gilligan after the island collapsed, and a colossal crystal dragon was coming up out of the sea. It was on its way to destroy London. Cornelia said sorting that out was her job, not ours, and then she switched us off.//

Brzk909 thanked her, then went on, //Ridiculous as all of that sounds, I will take your word for it. We need to find out what happened next.//

They climbed on, trying to ignore the shouts, sirens and commands coming from lower down the tower. There was nothing they could do except get on with the job in hand. *There* was the confrontation with the crystal wizard, and *there* was Cornelia Gilligan's rescue. No time to study any of these memories – they were signposts glimpsed on the information highway up which they drove at high speed.

But here at last was the memory of the moment at which Cornelia switched off their slowsuits.

//Here we are,// sent Brzk909, flashing for Veronique to slow down.

The next memory which was clearly hers (as opposed to Faben-Dah-237a's) showed her arriving back in the cybernet, just as she had been, what seemed like a million fractions ago, when Veronique had called out for her help. No sign of Veronique in this memory – perhaps, unfamiliar with the cybernet, she had been drawn straight into the webnoid and trapped there. The mirrored memories were not continuous, and there were clear gaps. Moving slowly up this data tower, she saw herself back at her own, uploading her records of the island adventure. Then, further up, a memory of reporting to a server. It seemed angry, and she seemed to be explaining herself. Making excuses? The mirrored data was incomplete, the communications between herself and the server incomprehensible.

//This is very frustrating,// sent Brzk909. //What were we talking about?//

Veronique sent nothing; she had nothing to send.

The system administrators were getting closer now. There were many more of them this time, and their stream interrupters were out, ready to be fired once they were in range. With a rising sense of excitement, Veronique realised that the administrators had called in heavy assistance. Autocorrects were rising up towards them on all sides, weighty with digital weaponry and shining with malignant wrath. A half dozen system administrators were logged into each, interrupters at the ready.

//Oh, blinking 'eck,// she sent to Brzk909. //Are you making progress? They'll have us in a minute. It's beginning to look a lot like Christmas, and we're the prize turkeys.//

Brzk909 was too engrossed in her lost memories to respond. Here she was now, returning to her data tower, making one final upload, then climbing it, just as she was climbing this one. What had she been doing? She really was a criminal, it seemed! There was a break in the mirrored information at that point, but a little further up she saw herself on the very summit of the data tower, extruding a long spike into it, and breaking it off. She saw herself point at that spike, then self-consciously point with her upper trapezoid at this tower, the one she was now climbing, the backup that belonged to Faben-Dah-237a!

And there the mirrored memories came to an end.

From then on it was all Faben-Dah-237a. Happy memories of tidied bytes and deleted scraps, of visits from the derivatives, of interfaces with interesting partners, of evenings of art and mornings of research, of a program's life well spent.

Unlike hers, it seemed.

//We need to get to the top,// she sent to Veronique. //I think I may have left a message there for myself. Though I'm not at all sure I want to scan it.//

Somehow they made it. But there was no way to escape. Surrounded by a ring of system administrators with stream interrupters at the ready, covered by the autocorrects hovering overstream with their passengers, it looked bleak for Veronique and Brzk909.

//I'm sorry for all this,// sent Brzk909. //I don't know what I was doing, but I should have kept you out of it.//

//Nonsense,// sent Veronique. //We are friends. I could never be out of it.// She held out a virtual hand and placed it on Brzk909's middle trapezoid.

//All very fascinating,// sent Hod-23-zoop, no trace of kindness in her communications now. //But I don't care. Either you turn yourselves in or you are deleted. Make a choice.//

Veronique pointed to the data spike embedded in the top of Faben-Dah-237a's data tower. //Don't you want to know what it says? I know I do.//

Brzk909 scanned her surroundings. There was no surviving this. Whatever she had done to her data tower, she would never again be allowed her autonomy. This data spike, now the system administrators knew of its existence, would be carefully extracted, and probably destroyed. If she wanted to know what this was all about, this was her only chance. She flattened her lower trapezoid upon the spike and waited for her stream to be permanently, irreversibly interrupted.

The Quarterly Review

Reviews by
Stephen Theaker,
Douglas J. Ogurek
and Jacob Edwards

Audio

The Brenda and Effie Mysteries: The Woman in a Black Beehive

Review by Stephen Theaker

A 92 minute audio drama about the new adventures of the elderly Bride of Frankenstein, now going by the name of Brenda and played brilliantly by Anne Reid. The story begins soon after Brenda buys her small bed and breakfast in Whitby, and the first scene proper is when she meets "spiky old lady" and future best friend Effie for the first time. Their friendship is rather forced by a musical feline haunting, thought to stem from the epic fish and chips war between Cod Almighty and A Salt and Battery – but other supernatural forces are at work. Written by Paul Magrs, it's similar in style to the entertaining Tom Baker stories he wrote for BBC Audio, the story told on the whole by a first person narrator, with sound effects and snippets of dialogue when appropriate. The spirit of the novel series (reviews of *Hell's Belles!* and *The Bride That Time Forgot* can be found in #34 and #38) is here in buckets. Though the novel I read didn't totally knock me out, I still enjoyed this audio version. A good start to the series. ★★★☆☆

Half a King

Review by Stephen Theaker

Young Yarvi becomes king after his father and brother are killed. He was born with one bad hand, and is no great shakes as a swordsman. He hasn't even practised it for years – he was in training instead to become his brother's adviser. He doesn't fit the mould of a great

warrior king, and on a raid to punish the supposed murderers, unhappy at the resulting carnage, he is himself betrayed. He survives, only to become a slave among strangers, an oarsman on a trading boat captained by a fabulous grotesque who constantly chides herself for her soft heart. Will his knowledge and cleverness be enough to keep him alive in a violent world? And if he can stay alive, can he get his vengeance? What compromises and sacrifices is he willing to make? This is **Half a King** (Harper Audio, digital audiobook, 9 hrs 26 mins), an audiobook written by Joe Abercrombie and read by Ben Elliott. The reading is good, though after hearing Steven Pacey's work on other books by Joe Abercrombie you can't help missing it here. It's much shorter than some of the author's other novels; the audiobook of *The Heroes* lasts twenty-three hours. That the book sticks with Yarvi's point of view makes it perfect for audio, because it's always easy to pick up where you are. It's not a work of great originality, but it's well done, and I enjoyed it, and people who have enjoyed this kind of story before will probably enjoy it once again. It will go down a storm in school libraries. It asks interesting questions about the workings of its own plot, the things we might take for granted: that the deposed king must fight his way back to power, and that we should support him as he does. Yarvi's actions could cause the deaths of his own people, and in the end, for what? That he should be king instead of someone else? Really, it's revenge, he's made a vow, and there's a strong sense that everyone else would have been better off if he hadn't. The plot is very well worked, with motivations clicking into place at the end. The twists are excellent, and even if this was planned as the first of a trilogy it works well as a standalone novel; little is left up in the air except the pleasant possibility of future conflicts and revenges. ★★★☆☆

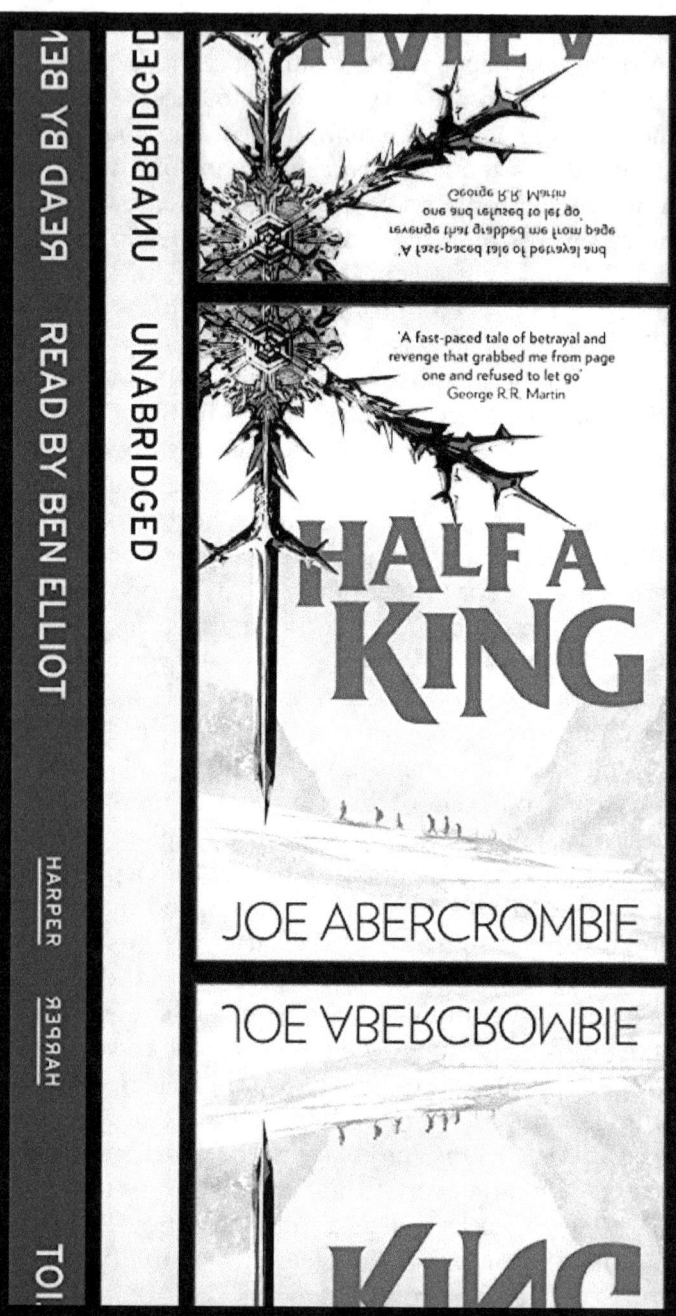

Books

The Forever Watch

Review by Jacob Edwards

First up, the funambulist.

Entrenched within the *Noah*, an unimaginably vast city-spaceship, the remnants of mankind trek obdurately through space *en route* to a new home-world. Adults labour for the common cause, enduring whatever stringencies are necessary. Children are raised by the state, the course of their lives determined by aptitude tests and the latent strength of their psychic abilities. Hundreds of generations pass. The mission is everything. Yet, for all she has been indoctrinated to believe that species survival is paramount, telekinesist Hana Dempsey, suddenly at odds with the power-elite who run the ship, finds herself embroiled in an unsanctioned hunt for a serial killer who shouldn't exist but whose grisly touch ghosts across the *Noah*'s Nth Web, hinting at a conspiracy beyond nightmare.

In terms of concept, debut novelist David Ramirez with *The Forever Watch* (Hodder & Stoughton, 326pp) sets out to walk a tightrope. Stylistically, he does so without a safety net. There are some wobbles along the way, yet by the end of the book there can be little doubt that, should he be able to repeat and build on the performance, he will garner sufficient reputation to secure a future in the profession.

The Forever Watch is written in the present tense, which from the outset puts it in an odd minority. The shift in perspective requires a degree of acclimatisation – from both reader and writer; Ramirez sways woozily on a few occasions when shuffling from absolute to relative tense – but soon ceases to be a distraction. There is a sense of immediacy to eyewitness accounts presented in this way, particularly as Ramirez favours short sentences; the story is told through small blocks of thought, almost as if unfolding in real time.

Further to the boldness of making a novel-length foray in the present tense, Ramirez transplants his authorial voice into a female protagonist for the first person narrative. Male writers have been (collectively) accused of underrepresenting women in science fiction. Ramirez therefore deserves credit for placing Hana Dempsey at the crux of his world; but of course, in doing so he lays himself open to all manner of possible criticisms as to the fidelity of his depiction. The men in the story are themselves a mixed bag: minor character Hennessy, for example, is given a certain depth, whereas Barrens (second billed behind Dempsey) is somewhat stereotyped to cyberpunk preconceptions and speaks in a jarring, unwarrantable pulp-detective patois. The characterisation of Hana serves perfectly well in the gender-neutral sense of moving the plot forwards; for some readers, however, judgment of *The Forever Watch* may ultimately come down to a verdict on whether Ramirez's portrayal of her is closer to creditable or culpable.

One undeniable strength of Ramirez's work is his imagining of the *Noah*'s insular, pseudo-totalitarian society, the basic framework of which is established via an adroit series of flashbacks to earlier in Hana's life (still written in the present tense) and then fleshed out as events unfold in the here and now. The world of *The Forever Watch* is vividly realised and integral to Ramirez's story, yet has been unobtrusively (though very deliberately) brought to life. What is most impressive about this is not so much the creative vision but Ramirez's commitment to what he has put in place; rather than preserve his setting for possible

"Vivid, action-packed, and yet filled with scientific plausibility,
The Forever Watch propels you on tense voyage of mystery, surprise and discovery."
—DAVID BRIN, *New York Times* Bestselling Author of *Existence*

THE
FOREVER
WATCH

A NOVEL

DAVID RAMIREZ

sequels, he instead allows the scenario to play out in full, affording scope not only for a symbiosis between action and locale but also for a novel that is unusual in its high level of self-containment.

Having set off across the tightrope, Ramirez does falter slightly at about the quarter-way mark (there is a lull in impetus, which many will find off-putting), but he then takes a deep breath and forges ahead, letting the balancing act play out come what may. For all that each step follows the previous, the shadowy endpoint he reaches is considerably removed both from where Hana and Barrens started and from where we might have expected their investigation to lead. In what is a darkly satisfying, uncompromising debut, *The Forever Watch* sends an exotic, visceral shiver through the dystopian genre, and in doing so flags Ramirez as an author to be kept under close observation.

The Book of Iod: Ten Cthulhu Stories

Review by Stephen Theaker

What a surprise: if I ever knew that Henry Kuttner had written Cthulhu mythos stories, I had forgotten it long before seeing this book. What mad nightmares could spring from the imagination that brought us "The Last Mimzy"? Unfortunately, **Book of Iod: Ten Cthulhu Stories** (Diversion Books, ebook, 2187ll) is slightly mistitled, since Cthulhu (bless his name!) is only mentioned in passing twice. "The Invaders" is the most traditional mythos story, about a writer whose drug-assisted time-travelling for inspiration has opened the way for things that shouldn't be here. Kuttner's world differs from Lovecraft's: Cthulhu here is almost the hero of Earth, having fought off these things before, a bit like Godzilla. Not many mythos stories end with a human saying, "I felt a wave of reassurance. Suddenly all fear left me."

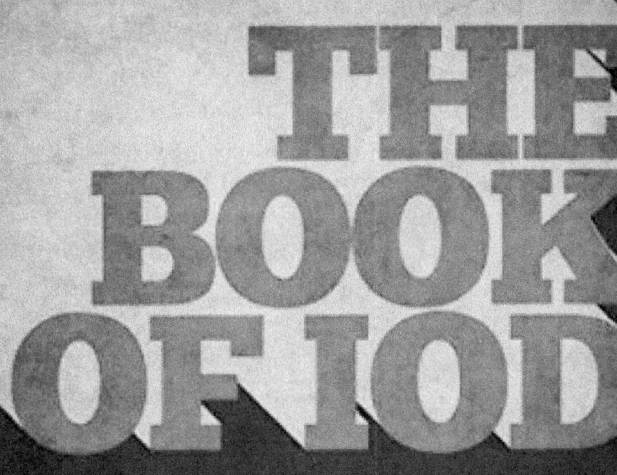

"The Secret of Kralitz" has a mere mention of the mythos. The new Baron Kralitz learns the dark secret of his family, in the course of carousing with his reanimated ancestors. "Spawn of Dagon" is a REHesque adventure where a pair of quarrelling adventurers are sent to kill a wizard, who turns out to have been protecting Atlantis all along. "The Eater of Souls" is a rather groovy story about the Sindara, the ruler of Bel-Yarnak, who goes to face a dweller in an abyss, while "The Jest of Droom-avista" describes the final fate of Bel-Yarnak. "Hydra" is about an experiment in astral travelling that goes horribly wrong, leaving an unfortunate expert without a head. The final image is one of the best in the book, but, as so often in this book, this is a story where, if you're clever enough, there is a way out.

Witches are a common theme. "The Salem Horror" is about a writer who finally finds the perfect place to write: a hidden room in a house that once belonged to a witch. The mysterious markings on the floor simply add to the atmosphere! In "The Frog" an artist wants the "witch stone" removed from the garden of his rented place. This foolishness lets out the witch buried there, who in the centuries underground has come to resemble her master (see title for details). Turns out that giant frogs are surprisingly scary.

"Bells of Horror" tells us of "the lost bells of Mission San Xavier". They are found in California and ringing them again causes all kinds of trouble. The most alarming part of this story is a toad that has worn away its own eye, scraping it against a rock to ease the supernatural irritation. Once again "the quick actions of one man ... saved the world". "The Hunt" is about Alvin Doyle, who wants to kill his cousin to gain himself an inheritance. His cousin has a cabin, and you can probably guess what kind of thing he has been doing there. Yes, "calling up an entity which mankind worshiped years ago as – Iod. Iod, the Hunter." The Dimension Prowler!

I think the present popularity of Lovecraft's work has little to do with his prose or actual stories and more to do with creating a shared universe in his stories, a relatively fresh alternative to the Christian, Greek and Viking myths, and then throwing it open to others to use. Sometimes, like here, his mythology is used in ways that don't much resemble Lovecraft's work, except on the surface. I wasn't crazy about this book, and the stories felt oddly optimistic, but I read it quickly enough and wouldn't have minded reading another in the same vein. Not the best Cthulhu stories I've read, not the best Henry Kuttner stories I've read, but still interesting to see the two interact. ★★★☆☆

Black Gods Kiss

Review by Stephen Theaker

If I were a judge and this were a court and the case were that of **Black Gods Kiss** by Lavie Tidhar (PS Publishing, 184pp), I would have to recuse myself, because by this point I am such a fan of this writer's work that my impartiality would be in serious doubt. *Cloud Permutations*, *Martian Sands*, *The Violent Century*: each has been remarkable in its very own way. If I were writing a list of my favourite books of the last few years they would all show up on it.

Fortunately this is not a court, not a case, and I am not a judge, and you are quite capable of taking my admiration for this author's work into account when reading the review.

Perhaps my favourite of his books so far was *Gorel and the Pot-Bellied God*, to which this is both prequel and sequel. Gorel is an "exile, mercenary, hired killer, thief, and what he liked to think of as odd jobs man", searching for his home of Goliris, which from the bits

we learn about it throughout the book doesn't sound so great. For example, in a wasteland Gorel asks what caused the desolation: "Only one word was whispered, sometimes, amidst the branches, in the falling of leaves." Goliris!

In the first story here, "Black Gods Kiss", Gorel acquires his addiction to the dust of gods. He is hired to kill a goddess, Shar, who has preyed on the men of a village. A kiss from her leaves him craving the essence of the gods. It is how they bind their followers to them, as addicts. This curse is at times of use to Gorel: its hold so tight it shatters illusions, as in "Buried Eyes", where he encounters a town ruled over by a sorcerer of Goliris.

The third story, "Kur-a-Len", is the longest, at about seventy-five pages, and is divided into six episodes. Gorel has come to the Garden of Statues, a colossal graveyard where "a thousand thousand graves gleamed as one", in hope that someone of Goliris may be buried there. In return for the help of the cemetery's caretaker in finding them, he takes on the role of security guard or sheriff, and must deal with both dead and living troublemakers.

The fourth story is the shortest, "The Dead Leaves". Gorel takes his guns to kill a man in the Deadlands, paid with god's dust by a sorcerer who sacrifices his life so that Gorel might rescue his daughter. In the fifth story, "White Queen", he gets involved in a messed-up version of the Snow White story.

He doesn't find his way home, not in this book – some say the world he is lost in is infinite – but he finds a few clues, gets his fix, and has a lot of well-written sex. Gorel isn't picky: gods, queens, ghouls and zombies all get their turn, even though it doesn't always do the trick: "Sex was sex and it did not fulfil him. Nothing did but the Black Kiss".

Pot-Bellied God was subtitled a "Guns & Sorcery

Novella", and that's what this is, classic heroic fantasy with a hero as selfish as Conan, as miserable as Elric and as crafty as the Gray Mouser, but who carries a pair of guns instead of a sword: "fine, hand crafted things, with grips of dark, strong wood and the small, exquisitely wrought silver pattern of a seven-pointed star on each: the ancient sign of Goliris." There are similarities too with Stephen King's gunslinger from the Dark Tower: the episode in which that character fought an entire town would have fit into this volume very neatly. If you liked that, you'll probably enjoy this.

The writing is as good as in Tidhar's other books, the atmosphere murky and groggy, the language thick and sticky. Gorel swears, which always seems surprising though it shouldn't. It's not unusual for dialogue from different characters to appear in the same paragraph, and even in the same sentence – lazy readers should be on their guard. My overwhelming feeling upon reading it is gratitude that such an exceptional writer chooses to write the kind of books I want to read. And if that sounds too gushy, you can't say you weren't warned! ★★★★★

Comics

Zenith: Phase One

Review by Stephen Theaker

It is 1987. Zenith is a pop star superhero who has never bothered learning to fight; there are no super-villains, so why bother? His closest friend seems to be his agent, and his power levels are determined by his biorhythms, so they are careful to schedule public appearances for the right time of the month. The only cloud in his bright blue sky is that he doesn't know what happened to his parents, Dr Beat and White Heat.

Or at least that was the only cloud, until the return of Masterman, the Nazi superman last seen when the US dropped an atomic bomb on Berlin in 1944. Turns out he wasn't so much a superman as the vessel for a dark god come down from overspace, and the Order of the Black Sun have now prepared a new, even more powerful body for it. Zenith will need the help of what's left of the last generation of superheroes to survive the coming battle.

This comics collection was previously published by Titan in the eighties but Zenith, like his close cousin Miracleman, then went out of print for a long time, there being questions over rights and ownership. That made it one of the few Grant Morrison stories that I hadn't yet read in full, and I appreciate it being available even while hoping no one's rights are being trampled. In the context of his career it can be seen as leading neatly into both the superhero work and the weirder stuff.

Steve Yeowell's art is mostly in black and white, as was usual for *2000AD* at the time this story appeared (progs 535 to 550), though one significant page towards the end appears in full colour to excellent effect. It's not quite as good as his later art, but it tells the story well and excels when portraying the more otherworldly elements, like the creatures from beyond and the hallucinations of hero hippie turned Tory cabinet member Mandala. ★★★☆☆

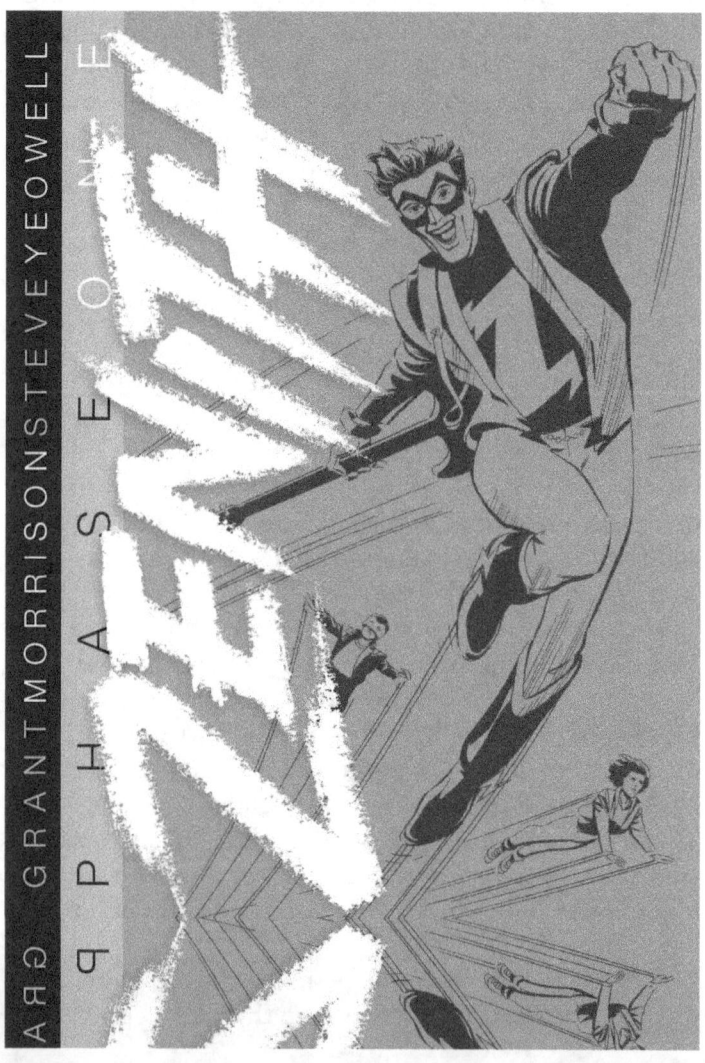

Films

The Hobbit: The Battle of the Five Armies

Review by Douglas J. Ogurek

Epic trilogy closes with brutality and finesse. If you're seeing this film in the cinema, do not buy a giant soda: there is no good time to go to the loo.

The dragon Smaug is pissed. The Dwarves have banished him from the treasure-filled Lonely Mountain that he stole from their ancestors. Now the fires rage in Smaug's belly as he approaches the human-occupied Lake-town to take out some of his frustration. Thus begins a riveting opening sequence that will set the tone for the final installment of director Peter Jackson's Hobbit trilogy.

The film's title, **The Hobbit: The Battle of the Five Armies**, makes a hefty promise: there aren't just two, three, or even four armies destined to clash. This is J.R.R. Tolkien, and this is epic fantasy in which the fate of the world is in jeopardy. So in the end, five armies will go at it! And Peter Jackson continues to deliver what he has brought in all his adaptations of Tolkien's classics since the Fellowship of the Ring first gathered back in 2001: acts of valour and treachery, displays of inhuman (Elven, to be precise) agility, seemingly insurmountable obstacles overcome, and speeches that, despite the often small stature of their speakers, deliver a wallop.

Word has spread that Smaug has left the treasure. Now everyone wants a piece. The Men of Lake-town want the share that Thorin Oakenshield, leader of the Dwarf band now holed up in the Lonely Mountain, promised. The Elves want to reclaim a handful of gems

(also in the mountain) sacred to their race. And unbeknownst to most, the ruffian Azog is leading a massive Orc army to the Lonely Mountain. Dwarves, Elves, Men, Orcs, and a mysterious fifth army. The movie builds toward the battle outside the entrance to the Lonely Mountain. It is coming, it's going to be big, and at its center bravely stands Bilbo Baggins, the series' namesake, in all three feet of his splendor.

A Thorin in Middle-earth's Side

Most of the fate of Middle-earth rests on Thorin Oakenshield, the heir to Erebor (i.e. the Lonely Mountain). There's just one problem: Thorin seems more interested in protecting the mountain's treasure hoard than he is in keeping peace or helping his Dwarf race survive. For all those who want to stake a claim to the mountain's treasures, forget it; Thorin is in the throes of the gold sickness that claimed his father.

Thorin's growing greed disappoints traveling companion Bilbo Baggins, jeopardises Dwarf relations with the Men and the Elves, and has the potential to allow evil to overtake the world. It's the money thing.

During discussions with his Dwarf companions and with Bilbo, Thorin reveals the extent of his depravity. His face alters as he tells fellow Dwarf Dwalin that he isn't above killing other Dwarves to get what he wants. During a conversation between Thorin and Bilbo, the camera shows an extreme close-up of Thorin as the film speed slows and he vows that he "will not part with a single coin".

It would take a monumental self-discovery for Thorin Oakenshield to change his ways, and monumentality is what *The Hobbit* films are all about.

More Great Battles

The battlefield action offers everything one would expect from a Tolkien-inspired Peter Jackson film: destruction, gigantic creatures, displays of bravery, and acts of cowardice. Though the full-scale battlefield action is enjoyable – note the contrast between the gleaming and orderly Elven army and the comparatively uncouth Dwarf army – what impresses most is when protagonists confront their Orc nemeses in one-on-one action. Watch for the battle on ice in which an Orc tries to crush his much smaller adversary by swinging a chain attached to a massive block.

At some point in the battle, the filmgoer is likely to question whether Legolas will enter the fray. Enter he does! From his transit into the action to his fight with a key antagonist, the Elven master bowman holds his reign as the most exciting character to watch in action. Best of all, we know that Legolas won't die: he's in the *The Lord of the Rings* adventure that follows.

It's Not Just the Fights

On the surface, this film is all about fighting. Note the film's title, or the posters that depict Bilbo Baggins brandishing his little sword. However, despite this heavy focus on physical battle, the fate of Middle-earth also hinges on a Hobbit whose true power lies not in battlefield skill, but rather in guile.

What Thorin Oakenshield wants most is the Arkenstone, a jewel that he needs to consummate his power. Thorin commands his followers to find the stone amongst the mountain's treasures, but Bilbo has a trick up his sleeve, or rather in his pocket: concluding that more harm than good may occur if Thorin gets the stone, Bilbo selflessly conceals it. This decision comes at great risk to the Hobbit, for if Thorin discovers the truth, he will likely kill Bilbo.

Bilbo also gives the filmgoer a character with whom to identify. When we see the agility of the Elves, the strength of the Dwarves, and the barbarity of the Orcs, we might feel as helpless as Hobbits on the battlefield. Martin Freeman's Bilbo Baggins, with his curious expressions and his occasional nose twitch, gives us a down-to-earth traveling companion who makes us comfortable and gives us a moral ideal toward which to aspire. Repeatedly, Bilbo proves his friendship to Thorin and to the Dwarves. Even when Thorin wallows in his gold sickness, Bilbo manages to evoke a smile.

The Journey Ends
In a brief scene near the end of this film, Gandalf the Grey (wizard) sits beside Bilbo. While the wizard taps and prods his trademark pipe, Bilbo twitches his nose and appears to struggle to find words. Their quest has been long and arduous. They have experienced major triumphs and major losses. These friends who started the journey to Erebor together decide to withhold the dramatic speech and instead, simply smile at one another. Some might consider this a throwaway scene, but this reviewer considers it among the most touching scenes in the series.

Thus concludes a trilogy made enjoyable in so many ways: music, maps, characters, speeches, conflicts, drama, action, creatures, costumes, setting. Perhaps some of us will learn from its central message: "If more of us valued home above gold, it would be a merrier world." True, true. But having a $250 million movie budget helps deliver that message exceptionally well!

Space Battleship Yamato
Review by Jacob Edwards

A wave motion gun blast from the past.

The animated franchise *Space Battleship Yamato* holds a similar place in Japanese popular culture as *Star Wars* does in that of America and other countries of the Hollywood-suckled West. Debuting as a 26-episode series in 1974, *Space Battleship Yamato* continued its interstellar voyage through two further seasons (1978, 1980) and spawned five feature films between 1978 and 2009. When it opened late in 2010, Takashi Yamazaki's remake – the first live action production of *Yamato* and a retelling of the space battleship's original mission – blasted *Harry Potter and the Deathly Hallows* (Part 1) from the #1 spot in Japan's box office.

Australian and American viewers of a certain generation will remember *Space Battleship Yamato* as *Star Blazers*, under which title the first two series were dubbed, edited and broadcast in 1979/80 (USA) and 1983 (Australia). Some of the adult themes were toned down and the character names romanticised – Kodai and Yuki became Wildstar and Nova respectively; the ship itself was stripped of its WWII origins to become instead the *Argo* – but *Star Blazers* nevertheless retained much of *Yamato*'s darker tone. Yes, Dr Sado was renamed Dr Sane and his drunkenness pitched as inexplicably zesty exuberance, but humanity remained on the verge of extinction and the *Yamato/Argo*'s last-ditch quest carried a real sense of import.

Space Battleship Yamato begins with planet Earth on the verge of succumbing to radiation poisoning, the result of a sustained bombardment by the alien Gamilas, whose armada has just annihilated the Earth Defence Force's last fleet in a battle near Mars. The situation appears hopeless, and yet a message is received from the planet Iskandar, offering salvation by way of a device to counter the radiation, as well as schematics for a warp drive and a prototype Wave Motion Cannon. Grasping at this straw of hope, the EDF dredges up the old battleship *Yamato*, refurbishes it with the new technology and launches it on the (series one titular) Quest for Iskandar.

Under Leiji Matsumoto the 1974 television series of *Yamato* was innovative in plotting a season-spanning narrative (rather than self-contained episodes), and also for its focus on characterisation, relationship

dynamics and expressions of conflict and loss. It was, in short, a mixture of space and soap opera, borne aloft always by Hiroshi Miyagawa's stirring incidental music. Along with the iconic visuals, these defining elements have, for better or for worse, made their way into the 2010 film. Composer Naoki Satō follows in Miyagawa's footsteps, albeit through leaving the seventies behind and elevating his accompaniment to a fully fledged big screen score, while director Takashi Yamazaki and writer Shimako Satō have honoured Matsumoto's predilection for strong-willed heroines: Dr Sado and Aihara (aka Glitchman) are rewritten as female, while Yuki/Nova is Tiger Squadron's ace pilot, whose first interaction with Kodai/Wildstar is to knock him down with a clinical and surprisingly hefty punch. As for the soap/space opera...

Live action *Yamato* carries a $24 million budget and the same glitzy, ground-breaking feel as did the original *Star Wars*, albeit it thirty-three years divorced from the cinematic context that would afford it an equivalent impact; and as much as Yamazaki's *Yamato* is about action, adventure, heroic self-sacrifice and one-in-a-million long-shots, it also dwells heavily on its human aspects and in particular the discord between characters. The supporting players all have individuality hinting at greater depth, but the emotional crux of *Yamato* is the strained dynamic that exists between Yuki, Kodai and Captain Okita (aka Avatar): Yuki sees Kodai as a fallen idol; Kodai blames Okita for his brother's death; while Okita perceives something of his younger self in Kodai and feels he must reconcile him to the burdens of command. Actors Takuya Kimura (Kodai) and Meisa Kuroki (Yuki) are both excellent, bringing real substance to their roles. Tsutomu Yamazaki (Okita) is unfortunately less expressive even than his stony-faced anime counterpart, but his explosive cries of "Warp!" –

rendered in English; a loan word, presumably, used here almost as a martial arts *kiai* – remain something of a highlight.

If *Space Battleship Yamato* has been diminished at all through transposition from serial to feature film, this doubtlessly manifests in the compression of screen time, one consequence of which is fast-tracked relationship arcs: as per the Han/Leia rapport, Kodai and Yuki go from rubbing each other up the wrong way to becoming life partners, but over the course of one movie, not three. The abridgement of *Yamato*'s outbound quest also throws up some quite odd emotional juxtapositions, such as when the ship is about to warp beyond communication range and the crew send their heart-rending final messages to loved ones: unlike in the more protracted voyage of the original series, this moment is reached within a day of their initial departure!

Yamazaki and Satō in fact evince a curious overall disregard for the constancy of time, especially where action or drama dictate. We have, therefore, a situation whereby the *Yamato* cannot take off quickly enough to avoid incoming Gamilas missiles, yet can power up her Wave Motion Cannon and so destroy these same, incredibly slow-moving warheads. Furthermore – and maybe there is some form of martial arts film convention being adhered to here across genres – the Gamilas ships and warriors seem always to break off their attacks if the crew of the *Yamato* need some alone time to work through their emotions. There are no detention centre arguments or "I love you; I know" moments played out amidst the action; instead, the soap and space elements remain clearly delineated and the poor old Gamilas have to sit around twiddling their second fiddles until the humans are done soul-gazing. The fact that the *Yamato* can, when pressed, twist and roll like a sparrow, surely is just rubbing salt into the Gamilas' wounded pride and their inability to bend spacenarrativetime. Truth be told, such manoeuvres probably looked less unrealistic in animated form.

Space Battleship Yamato is an odd mix, and would likely evoke both rotten and fresh verdicts if somebody were to set up a website (wince, *Rotten Yamatoes*) by which to critically review films with English subtitles. This duality is perhaps best captured by the inclusion, both in the end credits and in trailers for the movie, of the gravelly soft-thrash rock song "Love Lives", which Steven Tyler (of Aerosmith) composed and recorded having been shown clips from the final scene. It is a tacked-on piece of commercialism, about as congruous as dubbing the Village People's "In the Navy" onto footage from Darth Vader's flagship. For fans of the original *Space Battleship Yamato*, however, or those who grew up with the rebranded *Star Blazers*, such bafflements will be of little consequence. All that matters is that the journey to Iskandar at last may be undertaken again: re-envisaged in live action form and warped with some unmissable implications for the series' canonicity.

Glasses on. Firing the Wave Motion Cannon in five, four, three…

Jupiter Ascending

Review by Stephen Theaker

Jupiter Ascending is another visually stimulating movie from the Wachowskis, directors of such outstandingly pretty films as *The Matrix*, *Speed Racer* and *Cloud Atlas*. Mila Kunis plays Jupiter Jones, whose stargazing father died trying to stop robbers taking his telescope. She works as a cleaner with her mother and aunt, and they all live with her uncle's family, which includes a shady cousin who persuades her to sell her eggs for money.

But the doctors aren't after her eggs; they are sneaky little aliens in disguise, with orders to put her to death once her identity is confirmed. Luckily for Jupiter, just as she begins to lose consciousness a beefy guy with rocket boots enters the theatre, blasts the aliens, and carries her away: Channing Tatum, who spends much of the movie topless and glistening – for that alone this film will find many enthusiastic fans.

He plays Caine Wise, a splice of man and wolf, a flying soldier who had his wings clipped after chomping on the throat of an Entitled: one of the posh nobs who keep themselves young and beautiful by means of a regular "harvest". Caine is now working as a hunter, a mercenary, but he begins to develop feelings for Jupiter. There is no future in their relationship – she doesn't know it yet, but she is Entitled too.

After a spectacular battle among the skyscrapers of Chicago, he takes her to meet former colleague-in-arms Stinger Apini, played by Sean Bean, a human spliced with a bee, who lives in a house that's part hive. Another battle later and Jupiter and Caine are off into space, where the film's unusual structure will see her meet each of her three space children in turn. Well, they're kind of her children. Everyone is after her because she has all the same genes in all the same order as their mother, a grand matriarch of the Entitled, who in her will left the planet Earth to any recurrence of herself. (What foresight!)

None of the matriarch's children are particularly happy about her return, and as she passes through their hands Wise does his best to keep her safe, with the help of the Aegis, the space police, led by Captain Tsingh (played by Nikki Amuka-Bird, betrayer of Luther!) and the brilliantly named Phylo Percadium (Ramon Tikaram). Eddie Redmayne plays the most vicious of the three siblings, Balem Abrasax, spitting out his dialogue like Jeremy Irons with clothes pegs on his nipples. Before it's all done there will be space battles, fights with flying dinosaurs, last minute rescues, and romantic kisses in the midst of glorious explosions.

Any film with space police is off to a flying start with me, and *Jupiter Ascending* has so much more to offer than that. It is a beautiful, stylish film from start to finish, with special effects the equal of anything in *Guardians of the Galaxy* and locations so gorgeous Elrond would be envious. Wise's airskates are wonderful: it's great fun to watch him scoot around a castle or jump out of a crashing spaceship and slide down the side of a building. Some elements of the story are extremely similar to Jodorowsky's *Megalex* (see #50) and it does feel more like a French album than traditional American sf.

It could perhaps have done with being a bit funnier. What jokes there are tend to be underplayed. In the run-up to its release a lot of talk was about how daft it would be, thanks to Channing Tatum in elfish ears, but for me it could have safely gone much campier without going too far. Its locations and attention to detail may outshine *Flash Gordon* and *The Fifth Element* but it seems too anxious to avoid the giddiness and goofiness of those films, at least until its final, exhilarating scene.

I enjoyed *Jupiter Ascending*; it's by no means the hot mess some people expected, but neither is it the instant classic I was hoping for – though the Wachowskis' films do tend to grow on me. It took reading *The Art of the Matrix* for me to really appreciate that movie, and *The Matrix Reloaded* is now one of my favourite ever films, and would be for the highway sequence alone. *Jupiter Ascending* is a good film that looked fabulous, I can say that much for sure,

and it's a shame that sequels now seem unlikely. How much fun it would be to watch Jupiter and Caine fight side by side! ★★★☆☆

The Hobbit: The Battle of the Five Armies (take two)

Review by Jacob Edwards

Heigh-ho, heigh-ho, it's off to orc we go.

For many months I disavowed my ring finger's insistent tingle to review **The Battle of the Five Armies**. This was not because I hold J.R.R. Tolkien or Peter Jackson in any way sacred (although I do esteem *The Frighteners*), but rather because there seemed no way into the task. I felt, like Bilbo Baggins, too small to embark upon such an adventure. I hadn't even read *The Hobbit*.

Yet, review the film I shall, though many others have set out before me, better prepared and more assured of purpose. (There's even now in my possession a map marked *here be dragons*.) Review it I shall, even if this should require so foolhardy an act as to cross the streams, Ghostbusters-style, and write in the first person.

Someone once told me *never* to write non-fiction in the first person. It's advice I've taken to heart even while retaining no memory of whom so impressed me with the tenet. Their face is gone and so too the voice, leaving nothing but Yoda pastiche. "Review. Or review not. There is no I."

And why is this? Because there's too much danger of slipping into memoir (or, heaven forbid, blogging). This is now inevitable. I apologise.

I came to *The Battle of the Five Armies* having seen and mostly enjoyed both the first two instalments of the Hobbit trilogy and also Peter Jackson's three-pronged take on *The Lord of the Rings*. This latter was a book I *had* read, its three volumes bound together in one bitter pill and shoved down my throat at university as part of a feminism in electric sheep's clothing degree. I remember a distended week of Tolkien, mitigated only by old Tom Bombadil singing ditties about himself in the third person. I remember the lecturer perched like Smaug atop her pedestal, steaming with self-importance. I remember scoring exactly the same as my brother across three pieces of assessment, but notching a lower grade because not all assignments are created equal and marks out of 100 are not fungible. You see? Memoir.

I tried, having watched it on the big screen, to then read *The Hobbit*, but I failed. Much though the imaginative elements were there, the prose itself seemed laboured. It was like going back to Enid Blyton, only without any childhood nostalgia to sweeten the journey. I just couldn't abide all the descriptive repetition; the sameness of Tolkien's firkydoodling.

What, then, to do?

Thinking back to my English degree, I distinctly recall the feeling of reprieve I experienced upon discovering *Tess of the d'Urbervilles* as an audiobook. Rather than read it myself, I could listen to Martin Shaw, with whom I was familiar primarily through *The Professionals*, but also by way of a more serious snippet of period drama I'd happened upon one night while channel surfing. *East Lynne*, perhaps? "I should like to take a stroll on the moor." Hand to hip; britches and jacket. Something like that.

Martin Shaw made *Tess of the d'Urbervilles* bearable, and so I was pleased to learn in my more recent time of need that he could also be heard reading *The Hobbit*. Not every dwarf cloak is described – the audiobook is slightly abridged – but Shaw weaves his sonorous spell for a good six hours, narrating, putting on a plethora of voices and generally matching the film trilogy's epic sense of adventure. Dating from 1993, Shaw's virtuoso rendition of Gollum must surely have informed Andy Serkis' now-iconic performance across Peter Jackson's *magnum opus*.

And so, at last, to *The Battle of the Five Armies*.

Tolkien, it seems to me (speaking of his corpus of works rather than the man himself), is one of those rare literary phenomena where the story being told comes in some measure to be associated, either positively or negatively, with the circumstances by which it is read, heard or viewed. Preconceptions; personal experience; prior encounters with Middle-earth: everything goes into the mix and the film, in this case, either weaves its spell or it doesn't. Objectivity itself becomes subjective.

Which is my excuse for spurning even the pretence of critical analysis, and offering instead merely a conscious stream of likes and didn't-likes. Or rather, a list of *especial* likes and didn't-likes, which heavily favours the latter. As much as I enjoyed the movie overall, the best part was still picking it apart afterwards...

Starting with the good, we have Billy Connolly as Thorin Oakenshield's second cousin, Dáin Ironfoot, whose injection into proceedings adds some much-needed charisma to all the fighting. Regardless of whether or not Connolly would have tallied with Tolkien's conception of Dwarf royalty, this for me was the highlight.

Moving on to good that segues into bad, we have Martin Freeman. When it was first announced that Freeman would play the role of Bilbo Baggins, my reaction was the same as when he was cast as Arthur Dent; namely, "Yes. Perfect." Freeman brings tremendous nuance to the screen. He's one of those actors who can do a lot with little; who can *say* a lot while not quite saying anything at all. In the same way that Eric Idle's Nudge Nudge, Wink Wink sketch looks somewhat underwhelming in written form but comes alive in performance, Martin Freeman can take ordinary (or even quite trite) lines and make them thoroughly convincing.

Freeman, in short (hey, accidental pun), has bravura to burn. The only problem is that he's hardly ever on screen. Too many battles, not enough Bilbo! The same could be said of Sylvester McCoy as Radagast the Brown, but Freeman surely deserves more while playing the titular character. (Yes, I refer to the film by its subtitle, but all those armies aside, it's still meant to be *The Hobbit*.) Peter Jackson in this respect has been perhaps too faithful to the book, going so far as to have Bilbo knocked unconscious and leaving everyone else to get on with it. Yes, that's how Tolkien himself played it, but Tolkien also introduced Bard only minutes before Smaug was slain. Jackson saw no reason not to flesh out *that* character. Why then pay such little attention to poor old Bilbo? Presumably because...

...and here we move fully into the realm of bad points, *The Battle of the Five Armies* really is, by and large, just one big fight sequence. (And an excuse for Legolas to defy gravity; clearly he's one of those elves who, if he found himself in a plummeting elevator, would jump up just before it hit the ground and so escape all harm.) There's quite a bit of fighting in the book, too, but there's also a lot of downtime, which Tolkien had the luxury of passing off in narrative voice. "They rested there for several weeks," for instance, works better on the page than as a visual collage of dwarves sitting about the place, smoothing out their beards and generally recuperating. Peter Jackson omits such details and, cinematically speaking, this probably makes sense. The result is an uninterrupted narrative; but it's one where time and space are outlandishly compressed. Everything happens all at once. Battles are fought. New armies appear. Middle-earth becomes somehow very small, as if you could take it all in just by standing atop the nearest hill. The whole scenario blossoms and dies like a sunflower in time-lapse.

And somewhere amongst it all, the hobbit aspect – the journey itself; Bilbo's tookish adventure, reluctantly embraced and constantly at odds with his Baggins instincts – is lost, replaced by run-of-the-mill heroics and overplayed dramatic overtures.

And orcs. Orcs!

There are two types of orc: some are near enough indestructible; others die if you brush past them too quickly and cause a draught. And remember what I said about Jackson being too faithful to the book? I take that back. Yes, Tolkien had orcs. They appeared towards the end and were fought against in a great battle. Jolly good. But Jackson has made his trilogy *about* orcs. They're everywhere, growling and snarling and chasing and dying, just to add excitement (so-called) where film laboratory chemicals have eaten away all the subtlety. If Peter Jackson were filming the siege of Troy, he wouldn't use a giant wooden horse. He'd have orcs. Multitudes of orcs, crawling over the screen like maggots on a dead hobbit.

But enough grumbling. Suffice it to say that my personal journey to Middle-earth was made in the company of two Martins, and that my enjoyment of *The Battle of the Five Armies* – for such it was, mostly – would have been enhanced had Peter Jackson opted for a more Shaw-footed or Freemannered, not so heavily orc-castrated, production.

Okay, well that's just dire wordplay. I should rub that out. Replace it with CGI.

Oh, look: some more orcs.

Tech

Kindle Voyage
Review by Stephen Theaker

I didn't buy a Kindle Voyage right away. The initial reviews weren't good, and those that were seemed to come from tech reviewers who didn't give the impression that they would be using the things for reading anyway. The Kindle Paperwhite had been a huge disappointment to me. The touch screen worked better than the touchscreens on any other ebook readers I had, and made it a device you could hold in lots of different positions, but the name was an outright lie, the e-ink screen no whiter than that of the earlier grey Kindle with a keyboard. The backlight didn't make it look paper white, it was a ghastly green, and could never be completely turned off.

And yet I used it a lot, because our house is fairly dim, even in daylight, and once I had an ebook reader with a backlight there was no way Mrs Theaker was going to let me have a bedside lamp on at night.

That made me keen for a replacement, but distrustful of marketing promises. I wanted to see one in action in a Waterstone's before buying, but the Kindle table in our local branch has now been colonised by gift books. I might have gone without buying one at all if it hadn't been for the recent Fire Phone offer, which I went for, then cancelled, leaving me with a bad case of *emptor interruptus*.

When it arrived, my first impression was that the Voyage is essentially an upgraded – fixed – Paperwhite. Both children upon seeing it asked, "What's the difference?" The screen itself, when the backlight is off, is practically indistinguishable from the

Paperwhite's. The increase in resolution is difficult to spot – although comparing it to my very first Kindle, the big white one that had to be sent from the USA, the improvement is clear: the text on that one now looks fuzzy. There are no new fonts, sizes or margin settings in addition to those on the Paperwhite, except when reading pdfs, where you can now choose to slightly increase the margins.

With the backlight on, though, the improvement from the Paperwhite is obvious. The light is much more even, much nicer to look at; it glows rather than ghosts. I think we are supposed to keep the light of this one on all the time, since a new setting of Auto Brightness lets the device choose its own brightness over the course of the day. It likes itself rather brighter than I like it, and its fluctuations are often puzzling, but the effort is welcome. I'm torn between appreciating the light and regarding it as a cheat, an admission that these e-ink screens have reached their technical limits and are never going to become as white as the pages of a book.

However, the more I use the Kindle Voyage – and I'm using it a lot, my Paperwhite passed on without even a kiss goodbye – the more I come to appreciate its small improvements on its predecessor. It doesn't have buttons for turning the page, but instead has a quartet of pressure sensors, two on each side. Two are a few centimetres long, for moving on to the next page, two are mere dots, for going back – the latter are very difficult to find when reading in the dark at night. These can all be set to issue a tiny feedback thud when pressed. The result is the most immersive reading experience I have ever had, being able to go from one page to the next with the slightest squeeze of the thumb. Even when reading in positions that make the sensors hard to reach – or reading in landscape mode, where for some reason they don't work – the Voyage

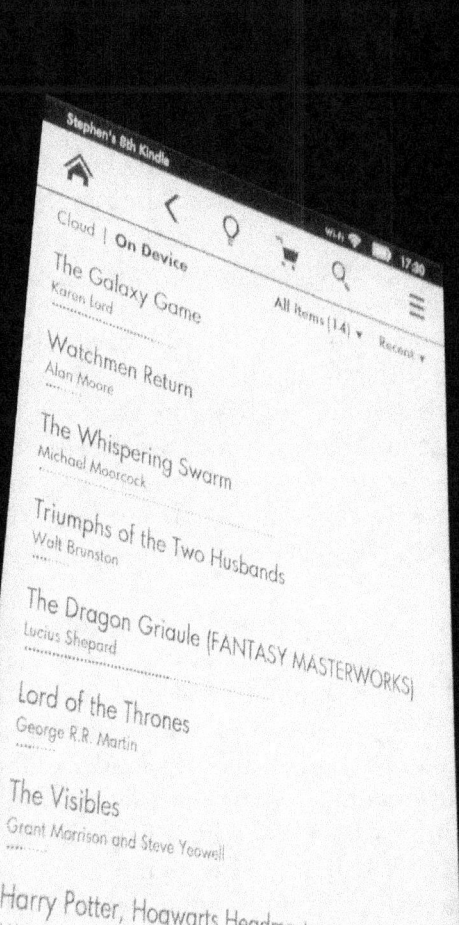

Stephen's 8th Kindle

Cloud | **On Device**

Wi-fi 17:30

All items (14) ▼   Recent ▼

The Galaxy Game
Karen Lord

Watchmen Return
Alan Moore

The Whispering Swarm
Michael Moorcock

Triumphs of the Two Husbands
Walt Brunston

The Dragon Griaule (FANTASY MASTERWORKS)
Lucius Shepard

Lord of the Thrones
George R.R. Martin

The Visibles
Grant Morrison and Steve Yeowell

Harry Potter, Hogwarts Headmaster
J.K. Rowling

1/2

improves upon the Paperwhite. Its screen is flush with the sides of the device, making touchscreen swipes simpler, more effective, and less irksome when reading for long periods.

There are other slight changes. All progress info, when displayed, now appears on the bottom left. When opening a new book from the Kindle store, a new About the Book panel appears, providing info about the book and any series of which it is a part, and letting you know how long it generally takes people to read it. The power button is on the back rather than the bottom, which is handier. The case gets quite cold outdoors. It's a bit lighter than the Paperwhite, and to enhance that I've made a conscious decision not to buy a case for it, because once the Paperwhite went into its excellent case it never really came out of it. I've gone back to the simple sleeve that came with the original Sony Reader.

Overall, then, I'm surprised by how much I like the Voyage, though its improvements over the Paperwhite are so hard to spot. It just fixes everything that needed fixing, and is very pleasant to read. If you'd told me when I bought that original Sony Reader that the top of the range ereader so many years later would see so few major improvements I'd have been surprised. Still no colour, pages still grey, battery power barely improved, music and audiobook playback lost... I'll read dozens if not hundreds of books on this device, but it'll take something special to make me buy another. (He says, knowing in his heart it isn't true.)
★★★★☆

Amazon Fire TV

Review by Stephen Theaker

The **Amazon Fire TV** is a nifty little under-set box that connects to the internet and allows you to access various apps and bits and pieces of online content, much like Roku boxes. Its small remote control takes you up and down through the categories – currently including things like Prime Video, Movies, TV, Games, Apps, Music and Photos – while left and right take you into the contents of those categories. The remote also has a superpower: hold down the microphone button to summon your entertainment with surprisingly reliable voice controls. (Text Search is also available in a pinch.)

The voice search shows up one weakness of the device; while working well, it only takes you to Amazon content, and much of that needs paying for. Unlike similar searches on the Xbox 360, results from apps like Netflix and the BBC iPlayer are not presented, and voice search does not work within those apps. That's a limitation that soon stops being a bother, as you get to know the situations in which voice search is worth trying. It helps of course if you have Amazon content to search for.

We began paying for Amazon Prime a few years ago to take the stress out of buying Christmas presents, and we would probably pay for it even without Prime Instant Video being included – but it is, and it is easily accessible on the Fire TV. People not paying for Prime will find the device much less useful, and will probably be irritated by its focus on Amazon video, but the selection is good, and getting better. *Constantine* may not be the classic we hoped for, but I'm glad we got to watch it each week on Prime, while the frequent Pilot Seasons of new shows are always a treat. It's nice being able to watch episode one of a programme without feeling guilty about not watching the rest. The selection of films is also good, though dig a bit and it still has the video store feel of the Lovefilm service it grew out of.

Prime Music isn't available in the UK, unfortunately,

but people who buy their albums from Amazon will find many of them available in the Music section of the device. This, for me, has been one of the greatest things about the Fire TV. Aside from a brief dalliance with Play.com, I've bought nearly all my albums from Amazon since I began working at home, and two hundred and three of them are available here. It's been by far my favourite way yet of bringing digital music into the living room. Playing an album can be as simple as searching for that artist with a voice search and then picking the album. Playlists can also be set up – we have one for each family member of their own albums, plus one for quiet reading – though that must be done elsewhere, such as a PC or the Amazon music app. One slight glitch is that the music stops playing when the television turns off, but that might be down to the settings on my TV.

Games on the device have surprisingly good graphics, at perhaps the level of the Wii. However, there are limits: *Grand Theft Auto: San Andreas*, though very similar to the recent Xbox 360 re-release, requires most of its graphics sliders to be turned right down before it will run on the Fire TV – not to mention that its huge file size takes up so much of this device's meagre space that it's impractical to keep it on there for any significant length of time. Other games are mildly diverting, and tend to be cheap, but have the usual tendency of cheap app games to demand additional purchases and apply penalties to gameplay when they are not bought. Games can be played with the remote control, or with an optional games controller, which is a passable imitation of the 360's. If I'm going to play games, I'm always going to turn on the 360 instead of this, but kids without consoles would appreciate the games.

Game and other apps bought in the Amazon App Store for Android devices or the Kindle Fire become available at no extra cost here, where a version compatible with the Fire TV is available.

Some apps are missing altogether, notably the BBC Radio Player, Now TV (reciprocally, Amazon Instant Video is unavailable on the Roku), Kindle and Audible. The last is presumably down to Audible being set up for downloads rather than streaming, but it was still a big disappointment. I'd hoped too for some kind of fun Kindle app – no one is going to read full novels on their television, but it'd be useful for family reading, exercise, and things like that. There is no Comixology app either – HD guided view on the TV would be great. NPR One and Spotify would also be good to have eventually.

YouTube is on there, and how much our household uses it shows one of the strengths of the Fire TV, that it is so quick to turn on and use. The 360 and TiVo have YouTube access, but going through the rigmarole involved in starting those up to watch a five minute video isn't worth the effort. With the Fire TV, watching the latest Jimmy Fallon, SNL or Jimmy Kimmel clips has become a very pleasant part of our daily routine. That the remote control doesn't need to be pointed at the device itself just adds to the convenience.

Any negatives other than those already mentioned? It lacks an on-off button, so crashes mean pulling out the power cord, Spectrum-style. For some reason, the film *Tower Heist*, having once been added to our watchlist, now refuses to be removed from it. And the option to remove a recommended film from display seems to only have a temporary effect. So let's say, for the sake of argument, not from any personal experience or anything, that in a moment of weakness a fellow was to watch a certain kind of film from the seventies, its sleazy ilk would pop up in his recommendations over and over as if he were playing a game of whack-a-mole. The only solution is to watch enough wholesome items to take the recommendations in a less embarrassing direction.

Another problem, but again one that may be down to my inexpert adjustment of settings, is that since buying the device our wifi router needs rebooting at least once a day. Whether this is down to the device, or just down to it encouraging us to stream much more video wirelessly than usual, is yet to be investigated. I have seen reports of other users having similar problems, relating to its screensaver streaming photographs from the Amazon Cloud.

That feature has been popular in our household. Again, we could do that with various other devices and apps, but it works so well and so simply and so conveniently on the Fire TV. If we want to watch Netflix or Instant Video or iPlayer or YouTube, the Fire TV is the device we now use. If you have Prime and a good Auto-Rip collection, I'd recommend it heartily. If, however, your music was all bought in iTunes and you prefer Now TV to Netflix, it may not be the device for you. ★★★★☆

Television

Supernatural, Season 9
Review by Stephen Theaker

The ninth season of this long-running series about a pair of monster fighters begins with the boys – well, men now! – suffering the after-effects of their attempt to close the gates of hell in season eight. Sam is in a hospital bed, in a coma, and the outlook isn't good.

The other consequence of season eight's conclusion was that all the angels fell from heaven, wings burning, thanks to Metatron's betrayal. One of those angels approaches Dean with an offer. He'll enter Sam's body and fix it from the inside, but there's a catch: Dean mustn't tell Sam. And so the two brothers are back to keeping secrets again.

The world needs the Winchesters as much as ever. A resurrected Knight of Hell is challenging cuddly old Crowley for the crown. Many angels died in the fall, but the survivors are not getting along and are looking for host bodies – evangelists are only too happy to help, even if half of those thus possessed simply explode.

This is another good season of a reliable show. I sometimes wish it'd move on from the angels and demons storylines, but when this season also features a Wicked Witch from Oz, werewolves preparing for Ragnarok, a guy who is experimenting with combinations of animal powers, and the return of Cain, the first murderer (played with wonderful intensity by *Psych*'s Timothy Omundson), you can't complain too much about the variety.

Part of the programme's longevity must be down to its ability to contain within itself a wide range of

moods, from tortured guilt and gut-wrenching horror to postmodern games (would-be god Metatron lecturing the viewer on story structure) and daft humour (Dean learning to speak dog, and in the process coming to appreciate a good game of fetch).

The one duff episode this season is "Bloodlines", a backdoor pilot for a proposed spin-off that didn't get off the ground. Showing the lives and loves of the warring monster families of Chicago, it seems like an attempt to do *Gossip Girl* within the *Supernatural* universe. That may sound daft but *Arrow* seems to have done well after starting with a similar premise. I won't mourn the spin-off, especially since *Supernatural* itself has just been renewed for an eleventh series, so no one's jobs are on the line.

Not sure how long it'll be before we get to see season 10 – E4 have just picked up the show, but aren't known for their timeliness – but I'm sure we'll wolf it down as quickly as we did this one. That's pretty much unprecedented for me with an American drama that has gone on for so long. Even *NCIS* (which has a similar knack of combining humour and high drama) fell off our radar eventually. But we'll keep watching *Supernatural* as long as they keep making it with this much verve and imagination. ★★★★☆

The Leftovers, Season 1
Review by Stephen Theaker

It has been three years since 2% of humanity disappeared, all at once, and still no one knows why, or how to deal with it. Justin Theroux gives an intense performance as Kevin Garvey, the troubled new chief of police of Mapleton, New York, a town which lost a lot of people that day. The previous chief, his father, was locked up after becoming violent. His wife Laurie (Amy Brenneman, giving a brilliant, mostly non-

FROM THE CO-CREATOR OF LOST AND THE DIRECTOR OF FRIDAY NIGHT LIGHTS
WE'RE STILL HERE.
SERIES PREMIERE HBO 6/29 10PM
the leftovers

speaking performance) has left him to join the chain-smoking silent cultists known as the Guilty Remnant, who don't want to let anyone move on from what happened. His son is in the compound of another cult (its leader, Holy Wayne, played by a terrific Patterson Joseph) when it is stormed by the authorities. His daughter Jill is still at home, but she is pretty miserable too.

This first ten-episode season apparently uses up the material from Tom Perrotta's original novel, and if they had decided to end it here, without revealing why everyone disappeared, that would have been fine. This isn't *Lost*, where finding out that kind of answer was so important. The mysteries here are how people carry on after something so awful, and why it's hit these particular people so hard, and those are fully, gruellingly, explored. That's not to say I wouldn't like future episodes to look into the disappearance itself. Indeed, my favourite parts were those that suggested supernatural agencies at work, and hinted at wider conspiracies, and if, as has been reported, season two expands beyond this one town, I hope we'll see more of that too, as well as all the other things the programme does so well. ★★★★☆

Constantine, Season 1

Review by Stephen Theaker

John Constantine is an English magician, exorcist and supernatural con man who at the beginning of the series is still an inmate at Ravenscar, an American institution for the mentally unwell, following the unsuccessful exorcism of a little girl in Newcastle. As **Constantine, Season 1** (and possibly the only season) continues, we meet others who were there that day and see what a state it left them in.

A supernatural visitation makes John realise that he

must get back to work, and on the outside he soon hooks up with Zed, a weirdly-accented psychic on the run from a religious cult. With the help of hard-to-kill cabbie Chas and the advice of an angel, Manny, they must combat the rising tide of darkness. Monsters and demons are abroad, and their powers are waxing. (DC fans will be intrigued to see Eclipso among them.) They will find allies, like the pre-Spectre Jim Corrigan, though not all will survive the experience.

I wanted to like *Constantine* much more than I did. I've been waiting on tenterhooks for a TV series based on the comic *Hellblazer* ever since I saw the possibility floated in *SFX* #1. It is a natural fit for television, with so many meaty story arcs to exploit, a compelling central character who doesn't need expensive special effects to get the job done, and relative novelty – it hasn't been adapted to death already, the one film so distant from the source material that if it weren't for the title no one would connect it to this.

Part of the problem is that it is so networky. It has that feel. John has a little gang around him all the time like a security blanket, and he has a nicely furnished base from which to work. Constantine isn't the kind of guy to have a headquarters and regular colleagues, but that seems to be what you need for a network show. Giving him Zed to chat with makes sense, since it gives him an audience for the kind of speeches that in the comics would appear in voiceover captions, but he needs to be more exposed than this, more vulnerable.

Matt Ryan's performance as Constantine is spot-on, though. It is eerie to see a fictional character brought so perfectly to life, although because he's nearly always with his friends, he's always performing, always on; it would be good, if the show continues, to see more quiet moments, more of what he's like when he doesn't have to convince anyone of anything. He is not yet

seeing the ghosts of those who have died for him, but one feels it is coming.

The storylines draw from all over the character's history. There are elements of Alan Moore's *Swamp Thing* (albeit without Swamp Thing himself, as yet), much from Jamie Delano's run on *Hellblazer*, and nods in the direction of Garth Ennis's issues. The American setting – and the American Chas! – takes a bit of getting used to. Of course, that's where Constantine first showed up in *Swamp Thing*, but a UK setting, even if it was just for an episode or two, would have gone an awfully long way towards giving the programme its own feel. At least Constantine himself is English, which is an improvement on the film.

Ryan's performance isn't the only thing to enjoy. The title sequence and theme music are excellent, and that's half the battle with any programme. As DC characters crop up there are signs that this could become the supernatural equivalent of *Arrow*. It wouldn't be a surprise to hear that the question of its renewal or cancellation rests in part on whether the creators can negotiate for the appearance of other DC characters – a second season featuring the Sandman or Swamp Thing or Etrigan the Demon would be hard to resist.

The best episodes are genuinely frightening, and none are truly terrible. I enjoyed it much more than *Grimm*, though it hasn't yet found its feet. I hope there will be a second season, but if there isn't I'll be disappointed rather than gutted. As it accumulates characters, and as those characters build a history, the stories gain weight, and eventually that could lead to this becoming a fantastic programme. The problem with a thirteen episode run is that it puts you in mind of how much better it could have been on a US cable channel or the BBC. And why the heck didn't they call it *Hellblazer*? It's a much better name. ★★★☆☆

Notes

Also Read

Notes by Stephen Theaker

I don't have time to properly review everything I read, so here is a round-up of almost everything I've read but not reviewed since our last issue. In #50 this section included some books we'd had in for review, as a way of clearing the decks and making a fresh start, but this time these are all either books I own or books already reviewed for other magazines. The credited writers and publishers in this section are taken from my booklist on Goodreads, and haven't been checked against the actual books, so apologies to anyone who is miscredited or missing.

Angel and Faith, Vol. 1: Live Through This (Dark Horse Books) by Christos Gage, Scott Allie, Rebekah Isaacs and Phil Noto. Vampire with a soul Angel did some stuff recently that he feels bad about, and he's trying to put things right. Naughty vampire slayer Faith owes him one from back in the day so she'll stick by his side, even though she thinks he's making a mistake. The first story sees them tracking down the source of an elixir of life, and the second brings back Harmony, still the world's most famous celebrity vampire. Enjoyable without being essential; I think Angel and Faith are both characters who benefit from a bit of offscreen time. Watch out for the spoiler for volume two in the artist's notes at the back. ★★★☆☆

Avengers Assemble (Marvel) by Brian Michael Bendis and Mark Bagley. Collecting a blockbuster mini-series where the Avengers team up with the Guardians of the Galaxy to take on Thanos, who's got his hands on a new cosmic cube and an army of Badoon. It's not too bad, and the artwork is good, but the story struggles to fill eight issues and Gamora wears an appallingly sexist outfit that looks like Borat's swimming costume. ★★★☆☆

Baltimore, Vol. 2: The Curse Bells (Dark Horse Books) by Mike Mignola, Christopher Golden and Ben Stenbeck. A story in five chapters, which begins with a betrayal in Lucerne. Baltimore searches for the vampire Haigus, who he first encountered on the bloodstained fields of World War One. ★★★☆☆

Baltimore, Vol. 3: A Passing Stranger (Dark Horse Books) by Mike Mignola, Christopher Golden and Ben Stenbeck. Lord Baltimore fights his way through five short stories, hunting for his hated enemy. ★★★☆☆

Be a Sex-Writing Strumpet (self-published) by Stacia Kane. Reading this didn't half make me blush. It compiles a series of blog posts on the subject of writing sex scenes, principally for erotic novels. I don't often include that stuff in my writing, but I'd read some sensible blog posts on responding to reviews by the author and wanted to buy something of hers. And it was useful to me: much of what she says can be applied to other kinds of action. It's good, though some readers may feel it could have used a rewrite to make it more bookish and less bloggy. ★★★☆☆

Billy's Book (PS Publishing) by Terry Bisson. A short PS Publishing collection of deliberately fragmentary and repetitive stories about a boy who has odd stuff turn up at his house, like giant ants and wizards and unicorns. They're okay, but it was a bit of a surprise at the end to see what starry venues they had originally appeared in. ★★★☆☆

The Boys, Vol. 11: Over the Hill with the Swords of a Thousand Men (Dynamite Entertainment) by

Garth Ennis and Russ Braun. Everything kicks off. Vought American take control of the White House. The Homelander makes his play. Black Noir is unmasked. And Butcher wades in with a crowbar. Very good fun. ★★★★☆

The Boys, Vol. 12: The Bloody Doors Off (Dynamite Entertainment) by Garth Ennis, Russ Braun and Darick Robertson. After the climactic events of volume eleven Butcher gives the Boys a three-month holiday, but Wee Hughie figures that something is up. The end of another terrifically entertaining comic from Garth Ennis. Each book has been a treat. ★★★☆☆

Captain America, Vol. 1: Castaway in Dimension Z (Marvel) by Rick Remender, John Romita Jr, Klaus Janson, Tom Palmer, Scott Hanna, Dean White, Lee Loughridge and Dan Brown. A thrilling book where Captain America is taken to another dimension for a lengthy stay, a dimension of monsters ruled by Arnim Zola and his horrible experiments. The spirit of Kirby is strong in this one. ★★★★☆

Captain Marvel, Vol. 1: In Pursuit of Flight (Marvel) by Kelly Sue DeConnick. Ms. Marvel aka Warbird aka Carol Danvers drops her swimsuit costume for a more practical outfit, adopts the name Captain Marvel, starts wearing her hair in an odd combover, and takes a flight in her idol's aeroplane to try and beat a record. She gets thrown back in time and teams up with a band of grounded female pilots. The cover art led me astray: I expected art in the line of Frank Quitely, but it's more like Dan Brereton. Good in itself, but not what I'd been looking forward to. Sending the character into the past at the beginning of a new series gives the impression of not knowing what to do with her in the present, but the feminism is welcome. The elephant in the room is that while Ms. Marvel is reluctant to take on the name of

her predecessor, he nicked that name himself from the real Captain Marvel, the Big Red Cheese, Billy Batson. ★★★☆☆

Captain Ultimate (Monkeybrain) by Benjamin Bailey, Joey Esposito, Boy Akkerman and Ed Ryzowski. Amiable all-ages comic about an old-time superhero who returns to action at the behest of a little boy. I liked the way the Captain was depicted in old-fashioned four-colour dots, but apart from that it didn't quite hit the spot for me. Likeable, but not quite funny enough. ★★★☆☆

The Change: Orbital (Endeavour Press) by Guy Adams. A novella by my former BFS boss about a young Howard Phillips (!) struggling to survive after a cosmic rip brings weirdness to the world. The main monster is great, a horrible mixture of man and machine. Looks like the book's been pulled from sale now – the series is being relaunched with a new publisher. ★★★☆☆

Deadpool Classic, Vol. 1 (Marvel) by Fabian Nicieza, Rob Liefeld, Mark Waid, Joe Kelly, Joe Madureira, Ian Churchill, Lee Weeks, Ken Lashley and Ed McGuinness. The early adventures of the mouthy mercenary, illustrated for the most part in ghastly Liefeldesque style. Marvel at its pre-Quesada worst. The book collects a pair of woeful four-issue miniseries which feature lots of shouting, contorted posing and bursting through walls, plus a couple of other issues. The final story, from the first issue of his monthly series, is an improvement. ★☆☆☆☆

The Death-Ray (Drawn and Quarterly) by Daniel Clowes. A short indie comics album, republishing a story that originally appeared in *Eightball*. After smoking his first cigarette a boy discovers that they give him super-strength; this turns out to have been the work of his father. He also comes into possession of a death-ray gun. Unfortunately his best friend is a very bad influence. ★★★★☆

Doctor Who: The Roots of Evil (Puffin) by Philip Reeve. The fourth Doctor and Leela land in a giant tree. That is a space station. That has been programmed to kill the Doctor. A neat premise, deftly handled. ★★★☆☆

Edison Rex, Vol. 1 (IDW Publishing) by Chris Roberson and Dennis Culver. This Lex Luthor type was right. His Superman *was* a dangerous alien with a hidden agenda, and Edison Rex managed to get rid of him. Now he wants to make the world a better place, but everyone still thinks he is a supervillain. A quick read. Text pages flesh it out a bit. ★★★☆☆

Edison Rex, Vol. 2: Heir Apparent (IDW Publishing) by Chris Roberson and Dennis Culver. Edison Rex is still trying to establish himself as a hero, but the former members of hero teams The Peacemakers and Teenpeace are suspicious, and he's not keeping a close enough eye on his allies. Enjoyable, but a bit thin: of its 139 pages, 30 are single panels with white backgrounds of Edison talking to ROFL, this world's Mister Mxyzptlk. ★★★☆☆

Fables, Vol. 16: Super Team (DC Comics) by Bill Willingham, Mark Buckingham, Terry Moore and Eric Shanower. Mister Dark attacks, and in response Pinocchio and Ozma create a super-team to fight him. Meanwhile the North Wind has resolved to kill one of the Big Bad Wolf's children. This is the sixteenth book in the series, and I've only previously read the first couple, but it was easy enough to pick up. Good story, with excellent artwork. Shame about the repetitive borders on the main story, which take up a lot of screen space when reading it on a tablet. ★★★☆☆

Fantastic Four, Vol. 1: New Departure, New Arrivals (Marvel) by Matt Fraction, Mark Bagley and Mike Allred. Slightly muddled collection of two separate but related titles, as Reed Richards realises he is dying and takes the family off to find a cure – without telling them. Loved the pages with Mike Allred art. ★★★☆☆

God Rest Ye Merry, Gentlepig (Beale-Williams Enterprise) by Tad Williams. A novella about an angel advocate trying to help out a werewolf client. ★★★☆☆

Guardians of the Galaxy, Vol. 1: Cosmic Avengers (Marvel) by Brian Michael Bendis, Steve McNiven, Sara Pichelli, Michael Avon Oeming and many others. This shows up as a 350pp book on Comixology, so I was expecting an epic in the style of DC's three-issue crossover *Invasion*. Sadly not; most of it is a series of single panel guided view strips; the real story is only ninety pages or so. Lacks the verve of the Abnett and Lanning series, but the art is nice. ★★★☆☆

Hellboy, Vol. 2: Wake the Devil (Dark Horse Books) by Mike Mignola, James Sinclair and Pat Brosseau. Rasputin's ghost gathers his followers to resurrect the vampire Giurescu, servant of Hecate, and in battling them all Hellboy finds out more about himself and the destiny others have in mind for him. Wonderful art and a great story. ★★★★☆

JLA, Vol. 1 (DC Comics) by Grant Morrison, Howard Porter, John Dell, Mark Millar, Oscar Jimenez, and many more. My favourite superhero comic of all time, I think. Grant Morrison gets such a great handle on all the big characters, while giving the outgoing cast an honourable, brave exit. Howard Porter's artwork isn't always anatomically perfect, but it's always exciting, like a lightning bolt across the page. ★★★★★

Joe the Barbarian (Vertigo) by Grant Morrison and Sean Murphy. A boy with diabetes trying to survive a serious hypoglycaemic attack has visions of a fantasy world where his toys are alive and in great danger. This was pretty good, but I found it hard going. I love Dave Stewart's colouring on the Hellboy books, but coupled with Sean Murphy's art style it created panels that were really tough to figure out. We return to reality too often for the fantasy to take hold. Still, the cameos from toys looking a lot like Master Chief, the Transformers, GI Joe, etc were good fun, as were the authorised appearances from Batman, Superman, Robin and John Constantine. And how long has it been since Grant Morrison last wrote for the Zoids? ★★★☆☆

The Last Demon (Penguin Books) by Isaac Bashevis Singer. Three excellent stories in a Penguin Mini Modern, two of them fantasy. "The Last Demon" is about a demon who relates his frustrating attempt to persuade a rabbi in the town of Tishevitz to sin. "Yentl the Yeshiva Boy" is about a girl who wants to study the Torah rather than get married and darn socks, and the trouble into which that leads her. "The Cafeteria" is about a troubled woman who survived the Holocaust but now sees Hitler alive on the streets of New York. ★★★★★

The Last Rakosh (self-published) by F. Paul Wilson. Jack, an experienced monster hunter, spots a dangerous creature at the circus: a rakosh, a cross between a gorilla and a shark. This one is weak, because it's being kept in an iron cage and isn't being fed properly. One hearty human supper later it becomes a real problem. I'd heard good things about the Repairman Jack series, but this story didn't quite sell it to me. We don't see what makes him or the series special. He seems to be a typical tough guy, and the story is told in a straightforward way. ★★★☆☆

Lobster Johnson, Vol. 2: The Burning Hand (Dark Horse Books) by Mike Mignola, John Arcudi, Tonci Zonjic, Dave Stewart and Scott Allie. Lobster Johnson and his team must protect a journalist; gangsters have recruited supernatural assistance. Terrific art and a great story. ★★★★☆

Lobster Johnson, Vol. 3: Satan Smells a Rat (Dark Horse Books) by Mike Mignola, Tonci Zonjic and Scott Allie. A collection of smashing short stories with Lobster Johnson battling supernatural spies, gangsters and gods in the thirties. I love that his in-fight banter is simply a series of curt ejaculations. ★★★★☆

The Portent: Ashes (Dark Horse Books) by Peter Bergting. Warrior wood nymph Lin returns from the spirit realm to find much time has passed. Her wood has been razed to the ground, and the land is divided between three warring parties, two of whom she has a history with: her former mentors, a warrior wizard and a witch. Lovely art. ★★★☆☆

Showcase Presents: Superman Family, Vol. 3 (DC Comics) by Otto Binder, Robert Bernstein, Curt Swan, Stan Kaye, Ray Burnley, Kurt Schaffenberger, Wayne Boring, Dick Sprang, John Forte, Creig Flessel and Al Plastino. I could barely read a page of this without thinking, what the hell, Superman? The description of Descartes' evil demon fits him perfectly: "as clever and deceitful as he is powerful, who has directed his entire effort to misleading [Lois and Jimmy]". Here are just a few examples. In "Lois Lane's Super-Perfume" he proposes marriage to Lois – and then takes it back. It was a ruse to trap some swindlers! In "Three Nights at the Fortress of Solitude" he uses a robot to spank her so hard she can't sit down the next day! And in "The

Cry-Baby of Metropolis" he lets her go through the terror of reverting to a baby while pretending he doesn't know she's the baby, to teach her a lesson about inquisitiveness! Sometimes he's astonishingly reckless: in "The Shocking Secret of Lois Lane" he throws two drill-saws at her head to remove a box she's using as a mask! It's so sexist: in "Lois Lane's Signal Watch" Superman gives her an emergency watch just like Jimmy Olsen's. She summons the Man of Steel to unstick the zipper on her purse... ★★★☆☆

Star Wars Tales, Vol. 2 (Dark Horse Books) by Dave Land (ed.). Enjoyable series of short stories set in all periods and places and plotholes of the Star Wars universe. The adventures of Luke's severed hand and Darth Vader's encounter in Cloud City with C3PO were highlights for me, but it's all pretty good. Shame that Dark Horse have lost the license, it looks like they were making the most of it. ★★★☆☆

Star Wars Tales, Vol. 3 (Dark Horse Books) by Dave Land (ed.). Includes two strips written by Garth Ennis: how Han Solo won the *Millenium Falcon* from Lando Calrissian, and the life story of the first stormtrooper sent on to the rebel ship in Episode IV. My favourite strip was Jay Stephen's "The Rebel Four", *Star Wars* in the style of Jack Kirby. ★★★☆☆

Star Wars Tales, Vol. 4 (Dark Horse Books) by Dave Land (ed.). Another good collection of out-of-continuity *Star Wars* stories, including some focusing on Mace Windu and, more interestingly, Darth Vader. ★★★☆☆

Star Wars Tales, Vol. 5 (Dark Horse Books) by Dave Land (ed.). Best in the series so far, including a set of stories from indie comics creators like Tony Millionaire, Jason, Peter Bagge and Gilbert Hernandez. I could have gone for much, much more than four pages of James Kochalka's "Milton Fett", the useless younger cousin. ★★★★☆

Star Wars: Crimson Empire (Dark Horse Books) by Mike Richardson, Randy Stradley, Paul Gulacy, P. Craig Russell, Konot, Sean and Dave Dorman. A surviving member of the Imperial Guard goes after a traitor, bringing him into a temporary alliance with the new republic. Follows on from other expanded universe stories where the Emperor was resurrected in clone bodies; a bit confusing if you don't know that. It's okay. ★★★☆☆

Star Wars: Darth Vader and the Ghost Prison (Dark Horse Books) by W. Haden Blackman, Randy Stradley, Agustan Alessio and Dave Wilkins. A very good story about Darth Vader, a young cadet and another bad guy protecting the Emperor after an attack on Coruscant by Imperial rebels, by taking him to recover in a forgotten prison established by the jedi to house the prisoners of war captured by one Anakin Skywalker. Makes you think a Darth Vader film would be a really good idea. ★★★★☆

Star Wars: Legacy, Vol. 1: Broken (Dark Horse Books) by John Ostrander, Jan Duursema, Dan Parsons and Adam Hughes. Set a century or so into the future of the Star Wars universe, when the Sith once more rule the empire. The previous emperor, who wasn't a Sith, plots his return to the throne. Cade Skywalker works as a bounty hunter, and he plans to turn in the former emperor's feisty daughter. Decent, not amazing. A bit depressing to think the new republic will fall so quickly. ★★★☆☆

Star Wars: Tag & Bink Were Here (Dark Horse Books) by Kevin Rubio and friends. A Rosencrantz and Guildenstern in the Star Wars universe. Not quite as much fun or as clever as that sounds. ★★★☆☆

Steed and Mrs Peel, Vol. 2: The Secret History of Space (BOOM! Studios) by Yasmin Liang, Caleb Monroe and Will Sliney. Felt a bit straightforward after the wildness of the Grant Morrison volume. ★★★☆☆

Steed and Mrs Peel, Vol. 3: The Return of the Monster (BOOM! Studios) by Caleb Monroe and Yasmin Liang. Steed and Mrs Peel are faced with the return of an old foe from the TV series, at least I think so – I've only seen a handful of episodes. Readable without being remarkable. ★★★☆☆

Transit (Image Comics) by Ted McKeever. Street punks, down-and-outs, religious and political fatcats, and assassins. Spud is in a subway station when a murder happens. Quite challenging. Archetypically eighties in style and subject matter. ★★★☆☆

Umbrella Academy, Vol.1: The Apocalypse Suite (Dark Horse Books) by Gerard Way and Gabriel Ba. A bunch of former child heroes reunite as jaded adults. I would not have expected a comic by the singer in a rock band (even one who invited Grant Morrison into his videos) to be as good as this. Reminiscent of *Doom Patrol* with friendlier art. ★★★★☆

Usagi Yojimbo, Vol. 13: Grey Shadows (Dark Horse Books) by Stan Sakai. The rabbit ronin travels to collect the bounty for Hosoku the Bandit on behalf of a friend, and while waiting for the money helps Inspector Ishida to investigate murders and corruption in a series of connected short stories. Great stories, and the artwork is clear, detailed and full of character. ★★★★☆

Valérian et Laureline l'Intégrale, Vol. 2 (Dargaud) by Pierre Christin and Jean-Claude Mézières. Volume two of the complete Valérian and Laureline, which collects *Le Pays sans Étoile*, *Bienvenue sur Alflolol* and *Les Oiseaux du Maitre*. They're a pair of space agents

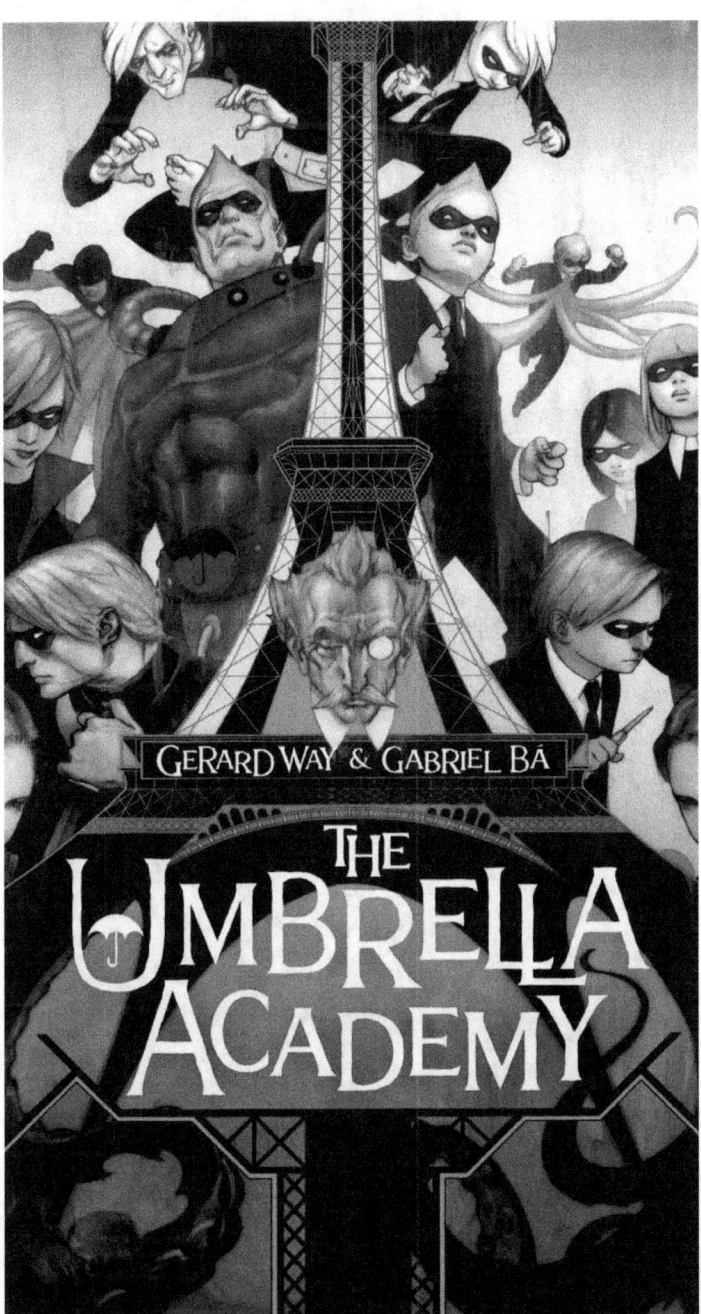

who get embroiled in a different adventure on each planet. Can't pretend I understood every word, but that didn't stop me enjoying them. I like how Laureline does exactly what she wants, however irksome that may be for Valérian. ★★★★☆

The Very Best of Kate Elliott (Tachyon Publications) by Kate Elliott. Reviewed for *Interzone* #257; I enjoyed it a lot. I think it might be her complete short fiction rather than a selection of the best, but I wouldn't have guessed from how good it all was. ★★★★☆

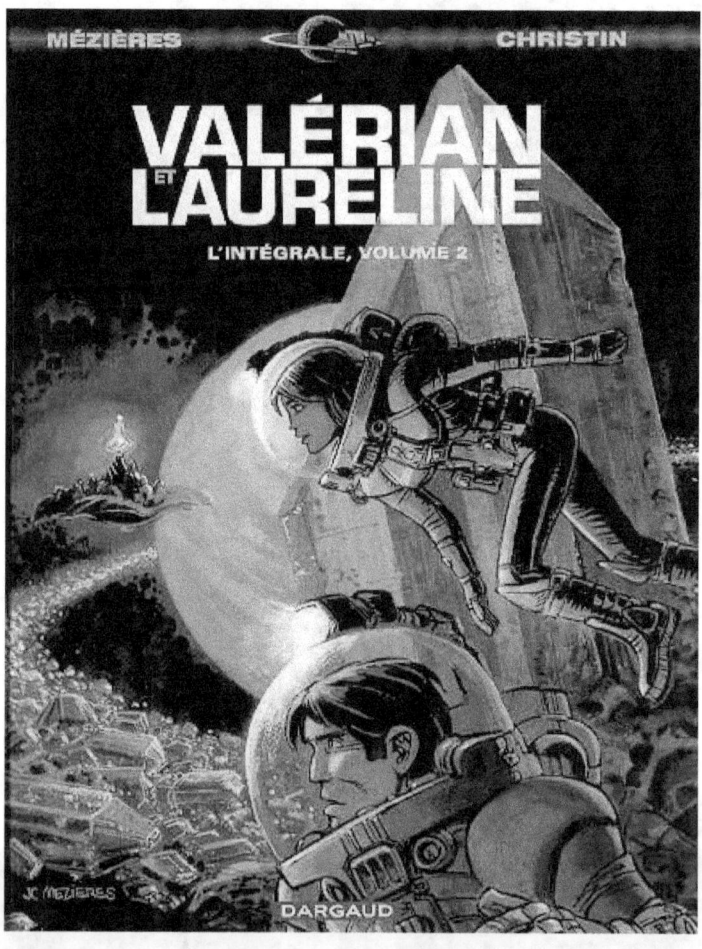

Also Received

Notes by Stephen Theaker

Print review copies have begun to dry up now, after I asked publishers to stop sending them to us last year. Makes me sad to no longer hear that exciting thud from the letterbox, even if I hardly ever got around to reading them. This section could disappear completely in time as more publishers move to systems like NetGalley, where you request the particular books you want to read.

Duchovny, David, *Holy Cow* (Audible Ltd): yes, *the* David Duchovny, and he reads it himself.

Hughes, Matthew, *The Compleat Guth Bandar* (self-published): ebook, received in 2014, but misfiled in my email till now.

Lord, Karen, *The Galaxy Game* (Jo Fletcher Books)

Magrs, Paul, *The Brenda and Effie Mysteries: Bat Out of Hull* (Bafflegab Productions): audio.

Moorcock, Michael, *The Whispering Swarm* (Tor Books): a new Michael Moorcock book! Will it be as good as the other sixty-one I've read of his?

Morrison, Grant, and Steve Yeowell, *Zenith Phase Three* (Rebellion)

Preus, Margi, *Enchantment Lake* (University of Minnesota): requested from NetGalley on behalf of one of my children, who promised to review it for us, but the review copy turned out to be a pdf so I'm not holding my breath. Wish NetGalley would start to say whether the files on offer are pdfs or epub files.

Smith, Matt, Arthur Wyatt, Henry Flint and Paul Davidson, *Dredd: Urban Warfare* (Rebellion): continuing the adventures of Judge Dredd in the continuity of the recent film.

Forthcoming Attractions

Expect **Theaker's Quarterly Fiction #52** in June, July or August! We'd planned to shift to a four-monthly schedule this year but we got this issue finished much earlier than expected, so who knows what comes next. Either way, the deadline for submissions is **31 May 2015**.

Most weeks begin with a new review on our blog: **www.theakersquarterly.blogspot.com**

Stephen tweets every few days or so at: **www.twitter.com/Rolnikov**

Going completely against what Stephen said in our last issue, the zine now has its own Twitter account too: **www.twitter.com/TheakersQrtly**

Our email address is: **theakersquarterlyfiction@gmail.com**